Odette's
Secrets

Odette's Secrets

MARYANN MACDONALD

BLOOMSBURY
NEW YORK   LONDON   NEW DELHI   SYDNEY

First published in the United States of America in February 2013
by Bloomsbury Children's books
www.bloomsbury.com

For information about permission to reproduce selections from this book, write to
Permissions, Bloomsbury Children's Books, 175 Fifth Avenue, New York, New York 10010

Photographs © Daniel Meyers
Italicized lines on p. 148 reprinted from *Jocelyn* by Alphonse de Lamartine (1836).
Poem on p. 152 adapted from p. 194 of *Doors to Madame Marie* by Odette Meyers.

Library of Congress Cataloging-in-Publication Data
Macdonald, Maryann.
Odette's secrets / by Maryann Macdonald. — 1st U.S. ed.
p.   cm.
Summary: When Odette's father becomes a Nazi prisoner of war and the Paris police
begin arresting Jews, her mother sends Odette to hide in the Catholic French countryside
where she must keep many secrets to survive.
ISBN 978-1-59990-750-5 (hardcover)
1. Meyers, Odette—Childhood and youth—Juvenile fiction. [1. Meyers, Odette—Childhood and
youth—Fiction. 2. Jews—France—Fiction. 3. Holocaust, Jewish (1939-1945)—Fiction.
4. World War, 1939-1945—France—Fiction. 5. Identity—Fiction.
6. France—History—German occupation, 1940-1945—Fiction.] I. Title.
PZ7.M1486Ode 2013   [Fic]—dc23   2012015549

Book design by Nicole Gastonguay
Printed in the U.S.A. by Thomson-Shore, Dexter, Michigan
2 4 6 8 10 9 7 5 3 1

All papers used by Bloomsbury Publishing, Inc., are natural, recyclable products
made from wood grown in well-managed forests. The manufacturing processes
conform to the environmental regulations of the country of origin.

For George

Il y a longtemps que je t'aime,
jamais je ne t'oublierai.

Odette's Secrets

Odette Meyers and her mother, 1942

∾ Rain in Paris ∾

My name is Odette.
I live in Paris,
on a cobblestone square
with a splashing fountain and a silent statue.
My hair is curly.
Mama ties ribbons in it.
Papa reads to me and buys me toys.
I have everything I could wish for,
except a cat.

Every day I push open the shutters of our bedroom window,
lean on the windowsill,
and watch the world below.
Today, rain drizzles down on Paris.
Nuns in white-winged bonnets hurry across the square.
Gypsies huddle in doorways.
Ironworkers sip bitter coffee and read newspapers at the café.
Life looks the same as always,
but it is about to change.

It's Saturday, so Mama and Papa take me to the cinema.
On the huge screen,
soldiers march,

their legs and arms straight as sticks.
A funny-looking man with a mustache
shouts a speech.
His name is Hitler.

Who are these soldiers?
Why do they move like machines?

Some people in the cinema cheer and clap.
Mama and Papa whisper together.
Papa shakes his head.
Then he jumps up.
He stalks out of the cinema.

Mama and I run after him.
"I couldn't breathe in there,"
Papa says outside.
"The air . . . it was like poison gas."
Mama rubs Papa's arm.

I hope we'll go back to the film,
but we don't.
Instead, Papa buys us warm crepes,

sprinkled with snowy sugar.
We walk home side by side,
in the chill rain,
just the three of us.

～ Cracked Glass ～

Sunday comes.
Mama and I go to the public baths.
We rent a room with a tub and a shower
for fifteen minutes.
I play mermaid in the tub.
Mama scrubs in the shower.
Then I rinse off
while Mama soaks.
When we're done, we rub our clean bodies all over
with scratchy white towels.
Mama kisses my nose.
Then she splashes cologne all over us.
Smelling like violets,
we walk home together, swinging hands.

On our way,
we pass a furniture store.
Its windows are broken.
We stand on slivers of cracked glass to peer inside.
Someone has smashed a mirror and slashed a sofa.
"Who did this?" I ask Mama.

"People who hate Jews," Mama says.
"The owner of the store is Jewish."

This makes no sense to me.

Are Jews different from other people? I wonder.

How?

I look up at Mama

and wait for her to explain,

but she just shakes her head.

Her Sunday smile has faded away.

She still holds my hand,

but she doesn't swing it.

Her shoulders sag

all the way back to the rue d'Angoulême.

Madame Marie at her sewing machine

～ My Godmother ～

Madame Marie's face is as round as the moon.
She's the caretaker in our building.
She lives in a tiny apartment under the stairs
with her beloved Monsieur Henri.
Every day she sweeps the hallways,
polishes the banister of our spiral staircase,
and takes in everyone's letters.

Mama and Madame Marie have been friends
since I was a baby.
They both love to knit.
They both make the best meals
from the cheapest ingredients.
When Mama went back to work in the factory,
Madame Marie began looking after me.
She doesn't have any children of her own,
so she decided to become my godmother.

Now, when I'm not at school,
I help my godmother.
We sweep and polish.
Madame Marie also makes clothes for me
and for other people in our neighborhood
on her Singer sewing machine.

I sit at her feet and sort scraps of cloth for doll dresses,
match up buttons that look alike,
and gather stray pins with a magnet.
Monsieur Henri smokes his pipe,
and the old round clock chimes on the wall behind us.

When customers come for fittings, they say,
"Oh, your little helper is here today!"
My heart glows with pride.

I'm always happy in my godmother's apartment.
It's so cozy and nice there.
"The heart is like an apartment," Madame Marie tells me.
"Every day you must clean it and make it cheerful.
You must have flowers on your table
and something special to offer guests.
If you make your apartment extra nice,
God will come to visit you too."

My godmother is like the perfect moon.
Always round.
Always full.
Always there.

~ Tea with Sugar ~

I just can't forget the shop Mama and I saw,
the one with the smashed window.
I still want to know why some people hate Jews,
because I'm Jewish!
Everyone in my family is Jewish too.
I decide to ask Madame Marie about this.
One afternoon, I knock on her door.

"Odette!" she says. She smiles her moon smile.
"You are just in time for tea."
I sit down at my godmother's table
and wait for my tea.
After I drink a big cup with lots of sugar,
I tell Madame Marie
about the smashed-up shop,
about the broken glass
and the ripped sofa.

"Why do people hate Jews?" I ask her.

"Some people in France today are angry," she tells me.
"They want to take out their troubles on Jews.
We will see the end of these people, I promise you."

My godmother is not Jewish,
but she seems so sure about things.
I eat another of her thin spice cookies.
I try to feel better.

∾ My First Secret ∾

Charlotte has disappeared!
Mama and I took her to the park.
My friend Camille was there.
"Let's go watch the merry-go-round!" she said.
Lions and tigers and horses whirled by so fast
we forgot about everything else . . .
but now it's time to go home,
and we can't find Charlotte!

I run and get Mama.
We look everywhere,
but she's gone!
What will I do without Charlotte?

"Such a beautiful doll," Mama says, shaking her head.
"Someone must have stolen her."

Oh, no!
What will I tell Madame Marie?
She gave Charlotte to me for my birthday.

Madame Marie worked a long time, I know,
to pay for a doll with a china face and real, curly hair.
I hate it that I lost Charlotte,

but it's almost worse imagining
how I'll tell my godmother about it.
Tears slip down my cheeks.
I hope no one can see.
It's almost dark.

Mama has an idea.
"I know!" she says.
"We'll keep it a *secret*.
I'll save money to buy a new Charlotte.
Then I'll knit a dress for her, just like the last one."

That might work.
But what if Madame Marie asks about Charlotte
while my mother is still saving?
What will I say then?

Lucky for me, Mama is a fast saver and a faster knitter.
Before long, a new Charlotte peeks out at me
from Mama's knitting bag.
This Charlotte has a china face too,
and curly brown hair.
She looks the same as the real Charlotte,

even though I know she's not.
As soon as her dress is finished,
I take my new doll to visit Madame Marie.

"Ah, Charlotte," Madame says,
"I think you need an apron."
She lets me guide her sewing machine needle
along the seam in the cherry-red fabric
all by myself.
But I feel nervous.
Will Madame Marie notice that this is a different Charlotte?
My fingers wobble
and the stitches come out uneven.
"Never mind, Odette," she says.
"Learning to make straight stitches takes time."
She smiles with pride at me
when I hem the apron.

What if Madame Marie finds out that I lost the real Charlotte?
Will she be angry with me?
I don't think so.
But I don't have to worry about that anymore.
Now I know a new way of solving problems . . . with secrets.

～ Different ～

"What makes us Jews?"
I ask Mama one night
while she brushes my hair at bedtime.
My family never goes to the synagogue
on Friday nights for Sabbath
like some Jewish people we know.
Mama and Papa don't believe in religion.

They like celebrations, though.
Mama makes cakes for Sabbath nights,
and Papa brings me treats . . .
books, chocolates, and toys.
I like books and dolls best,
but I pretend to like wind-ups
because Papa loves them so.

Are our Friday nights enough to make us Jewish?

No, Mama says.
We are Polish Jews because
Mama's and Papa's parents and grandparents
in faraway Poland
are all Jews.

Most of our friends and relatives in Paris are Jews too.
But Mama and Papa don't speak Polish anymore.
Our family speaks French.
And we live in Paris now, not Poland.
So why are we Polish Jews?

One thing I know for sure: we never have Christmas.
Madame Marie and most French people do.
Last December, Madame Marie wanted to give me a present.
A shopkeeper she knew stored holiday decorations
in a warehouse in our courtyard.
She said I could choose one . . .
a snowy village or a crèche.
I wanted the crèche!
I liked the stable with the mother, the father, the baby,
and all the little animals.
But somehow I knew
my mother would not want the Baby Jesus
in our apartment.
I chose the village instead.

We are different.
We speak French,

but we aren't French.
We live in France,
but we're really Polish.
All our relatives are Jews,
so we are Jews.
And even though we like celebrations,
we won't have Christmas in our home.
Not ever.

∼ War Comes ∼

One warm September day,
Mama comes to get me early from school.
"We're going to meet Papa," she says.
I am so excited to leave,
I don't ask why.
Mama and I go to the square
in front of our apartment,
the one with the green fountain.
Papa is there with his newspaper, reading.
He kisses us both.
His brown eyes, often shining, are serious today.
Mama sits down next to him on a bench.
"Go and play, Odette," Papa says.
Mama gives me some stale bread to feed the pigeons.
She and Papa talk in low, worried voices,
but I hear two words, "war" and "Poland."

The pigeons pick and peck
in the dappled light
around the splashing fountain.
I scatter crumbs for them.
Then I pass by the gypsies who are always there
and look at the statue of a man.
He leans forward on his knee

with his chin propped up on his hand.
Papa once told me he's called *The Thinker.*

What are his thoughts?
Is he worried about war and Poland?
Or does he wonder what I wonder . . .
why doesn't he have any clothes on?

That night, I lie in bed under my yellow blanket.
I rub the holy medals of saints stitched around it.
Strong Saint Christopher and brave Saint Michael
will keep me safe, Madame Marie told me
when she gave it to me.
Mama doesn't think this is true,
but she lets me keep the medals anyway.
"Your godmother made that blanket for you out of love,"
Mama says.

I listen to my parents' murmurs in the next room.
Here's what they are talking about: war, again.

I think the soldiers we saw on the cinema's screen
are marching closer now.
Are they coming to get us?

∾ The Dark ∾

I tell Madame Marie about those soldiers
and how afraid I am of them.
"I was afraid of things too,
when I was a little girl," she says.

"What were you afraid of?" I ask her.
She closes her eyes and sits for a while in thought,
her sewing in her lap.
Then she opens them again and licks her thread
to sharpen it for her needle.

"The dark," she says, "and big dogs."

"Oh, I am afraid of the dark and big dogs too," I say,
"but I am *more afraid* of the soldiers!"
Madame Marie's eyes meet mine.
Slowly she nods her head.
She understands everything.

～ Papa Goes Away ～

Hitler and his soldiers are called Nazis.
Papa can't wait to fight them!
As soon as the war begins,
he and Uncle Hirsch and Uncle Motl
all try to join the French army.
Uncle Motl has five children,
so the army sends him home.
But Papa and Uncle Hirsch have only one child each,
me and my cousin Sophie.
Before long, they are allowed to join.

I help Papa pack his things.
I put his gray socks and striped underwear and razor
in the bottom of the brown canvas bag
Madame Marie made for him.
Papa puts his favorite book, his blue dictionary, on top.
"When I come back," he tells me,
"I will know *every single word* in this book!"
I try to smile,
but I don't care about Papa's dictionary as much as he does.
What I wonder is,
who will read to me now from his *Encyclopedia of Learning*?
Who will show me the teepees of the American Indians,

the huge scary dinosaurs that lived so long ago,
and the twins and fish that hide in the starry skies?

Mama is always busy.
I already know who will read the *Encyclopedia* to me.
Nobody.

～ No Eggs or Milk, No Jews or Dogs ～

Aunt Georgette and my cousin Sophie come to live with us.
I like Sophie.
She shares all her outgrown clothes and toys with me.

Sophie and I listen under the table
while our mothers talk.
Fear is in their voices.
They always talk about the same things:
their husbands are far away,
and food is getting harder and harder to find.
We dream of eggs, milk, and butter,
but most of all real bread . . .
the kind we eat now tastes like sawdust.
Some people say it *is* made of sawdust!
"French bread," says Mama, with a groan.
"Only the *name* is the same as it was before!"

"Mama?" I say.
I know I shouldn't interrupt,
but I'm hungry.

"What now, Odette?" she asks.
"Can't you be quiet for even one minute?"

Then she looks at my face and she's sorry.
She gives my cousin and me each a cookie.
After that, she and Aunt Georgette talk
in their old language, Yiddish.
Sophie and I can't understand the words,
but we understand fear.
It's still there, in their voices.

Later, Sophie and I walk to the park.
A sign at the gate says, No Dogs or Jews Allowed.
Plenty of children are playing inside.
I want to go in too.
"How will they know we are Jews?" I ask Sophie.
She doesn't know, she says.
But she doesn't want to go to the park anymore, anyway.

So Jews can't go to the park now.
They can't go to the swimming pool, either.
A girl at school told me
Jews aren't even allowed to have pets anymore.
If I had a pet,
I would *never* give it up!
I still dream of having my own cat,

a silky calico with a pink tongue.
Not even Nazis can stop you
from having pets in your dreams.

~ Missing Papa ~

Before long, Papa sends Mama and me a photograph,
taken in his fine soldier's uniform.
The photograph is black and white.
Mama puts it on the table beside her bed.
I stare at it and stare at it.
I wish I could see the brown in Papa's eyes.
I wish I could see the shine in them too.

At last, a letter comes from Papa.
He says he's a prisoner of the German soldiers.
My papa, in prison!
How can this be?
Papa says we can visit him
in a faraway French town.
We must bring a cake and a box of cigars, he says.
I wonder why . . . will we be going to a party?
I didn't think they had parties in prison.

Mama barely has enough money for food.
My boots are falling apart.
But we make the cake and get the cigars,
just as Papa has told us to do.
Then we buy train tickets to go see him.

We meet Papa in a dark hotel room,
but Mama and I blossom
in the light of his smile.
He brings us pure castile soap from Marseilles.
We take turns smelling it in his hands,
the hands we have missed so much.

My family is back together again!
Nothing else matters . . .
not the awful sawdust bread without butter,
not my ugly, worn-out boots.
Mama and Papa talk and laugh and hug and kiss.
Things are almost the way they have always been.

But in the morning Papa is gone.
He has taken the cake and cigars
to the guard who let him visit us,
for one night only.
Mama rushes me to the train station before dawn.
Rows and rows of French prisoners march past.
Boxcars wait to take them to Germany.
Those soldiers, the ones we saw in the film,
guard them with guns.

I see my father march past.

"Papa!" I cry out.

He turns toward my voice.

Then a rifle butt slams into his back.

My hair prickles.

Mama's hand tightens on mine.

In a moment, Papa is gone.

I look up at Mama.

She stands motionless, not saying a word.

Her eyes follow the train as it rattles down the track.

When it is only a faraway speck, she sighs and looks at me.

I shiver and bite my lip so I won't cry.

"Come now, Odette," she says.

"We must be strong."

She buys hot tea for us to share

while we wait for our train home.

But even if she bought me my own hot chocolate,

it wouldn't stop me from shivering.

~ Running Away ~

The enemy is on our doorstep, everyone says!
That means the soldiers have marched almost as far as Paris.
Most people are afraid our city will be destroyed,
so they decide to run away.

Madame Marie and Monsieur Henri stay calm.
No, they say,
they will stay in their home.
Mama and Aunt Georgette can't make up their minds.
But at the last possible minute,
they throw underwear and toothbrushes into a suitcase . . .
we're leaving!

We run to the big train station.
On the way, I see the strangest sights . . .
a young woman pushes an old one down the street
in a baby carriage,
a man carries his dog in a shopping basket,
and a shopkeeper pulls his cash register along
like a child in a wagon.

So many people are headed for the train station.
When we arrive, it's crammed.

People try to get on any train,
no matter where it's going.
A sea of taller people hems me in, pushing, shoving, shouting.
Bryzzt!
A voice crackles over the loudspeaker:
"No more trains! The last train leaving Paris is full!"
People cry and faint and curse.
Lost children shriek for their mothers.

Somehow, Mama and Aunt Georgette and Sophie and I
drag ourselves out of the crowd.
We head to the subway, the *Métro*.
The scratchy seats, the squeal of the wheels, comfort me.
We're going home.

～ Bombers ～

Bombers fly over Paris at night.
Wailing sirens announce their arrival.
We rush into the basement shelter.
We huddle in the dark,
holding our breath,
waiting for crashes.
One lady wearing a lace nightgown
thinks she can hear them nearby!
But then the all-clear siren comes,
and we creep back up the stairs.
Our building is still standing.
We go back to our beds.

At first it's just once in a while,
but then the bombers come more often.
Each time, it's down to the shelter we go again . . .
until Mama hears about a building that collapsed.
People were trapped in the shelter underneath.
After that, we stay upstairs.

Finally, Aunt Georgette and Sophie can't take it anymore.
They have Christian relatives in the country.
They write a letter

asking to stay with them.
Before long, the relatives write back.
Aunt Georgette and Sophie are welcome.
So they pack their things and hug and kiss us good-bye.
They go to hide with their relatives.
Mama and I are alone again.

Sophie leaves me some colored pencils
as a going-away present.
I draw pictures of bombs falling on Paris,
of parks with signs that say, No Dogs or Jews Allowed,
and of trains traveling far, far away.

∾ What Dangerous Looks Like ∾

Everywhere we look now, we see soldiers in Paris.
Some strut past us, some thunder along on motorcycles.
Still others roar past in big cars.
They all wear huge black boots
and stiff uniforms belted with shiny buckles.
Some have lightning bolts
on their collars.

Mama says they are dangerous.
Most of them don't *look* dangerous to me.
They are young, blond men.
I see their blue eyes follow the pretty Parisian ladies.
The soldiers put up new street signs in German.
They take the nicest homes for themselves.
But they don't destroy Paris.
No, they stroll along the boulevards.
They eat juicy beefsteak
and drink red wine in the sidewalk cafés.
They buy fine French perfume
and pretty clothes to send home to Germany.

Some of the soldiers speak French.
They try to make friends with children.

They offer us candy.

"Don't take it," Mama warns me.

"Don't take *anything* from them, *ever*."

~ Lonely ~

Aunt Georgette, Sophie, and Papa . . . all gone.
One sad morning,
I meet Jakob, a Jewish boy I know,
on my way to school.
"I just got some toys from a cousin who left Paris,"
Jakob tells me.
"Let's go to my apartment and play with them."
I know I shouldn't skip school, but I need a new friend.

I go with him.
We have to be quiet and not turn on any lights,
 so the neighbors won't know we're there.
They would tattle to his mother,
"Your son was playing at home while you were at work!"

Jakob shows me his new toys:
trucks, tanks, airplanes, and lots of soldiers.
Some are German, some are French.
He lines them up on the floor.
"Do you want to be German or French?" he asks me.

"I'll be French," I say.
But I don't know how to play this game.
I make my soldiers do all the wrong things.

"Stupid!" Jakob says, taking my soldiers away.
"The French wouldn't fight like that."
He turns his back on me.

I wish I were at Madame Marie's!
She never calls me stupid.
If I were there now, I'd play with Charlotte,
make her a shawl.
"I'm leaving," I tell Jakob.

"Close the door after you," he says.
He dives his airplane down at the Nazi soldiers.
"And don't make any noise."

I have escaped the war!
I'm free!

~ My Mistake ~

I skip home through day-lit streets.
But when I run into our building
and pull open the door of Madame Marie's apartment,
I know I've made a *big* mistake.
Madame Marie's sharp eyes look at me in surprise.
She turns and checks the old wooden clock.
Too early, it says.
Too early for Odette to be home.

Shaking her head, Madame Marie puts a stool against the wall.
"Sit there," she commands me.
"Face the wall.
Don't look back."

I stare at the clock.
Its ticking goes on as though nothing has happened.
But Madame Marie, who loves to talk, says nothing.
Her silence is terrible.
I know I've done something wrong.
What if Madame Marie tells Mama?

After a long while, Madame Marie says,
"What did I tell you the heart is like?"

"The heart is like an apartment," I tell her.

"And how often do you have to clean it
and put everything in place?" she asks.

"Every single day, Madame Marie," I reply.

She picks up another sleeve, lines it up with her needle.
"All right then," she says,
"clean up the mess in your heart.
Take a good look and see what needs to be done."

I do what my godmother tells me to do.
I think about what I did that was wrong.
Instead of going to school,
I listened to a boy who told me not to go.
Jakob made it sound like it would be fun
to play with his toys.
But it wasn't!
And it wasn't fun getting caught, either.
I know better now.
I'll never skip school again.
I want my mother and Madame Marie to trust me.

My heart feels cleaner now,
and I feel better.
I take a deep breath.
Can I smell the flowers
Madame Marie told me about?
She turns from her sewing machine
and glances at me over the tops of her glasses.
Still she doesn't say anything.

"You won't tell Mama, will you?" I ask her.

"Will this happen again?" she asks.

"Never," I say.

"Then there's no need to worry your mama," she replies.

I have one more question.
But I wait a minute before asking it.
"What if Mama asks me about school today?"

"Then you must do what your heart tells you,"
says Madame Marie.

I sigh.

I know what my heart will tell me.

But I don't want to think about that yet.

"You can climb down from that stool now,"

my godmother says.

She bites through the thread she has been unspooling.

She angles it into a needle.

"Would you like to learn how to sew on a button?"

What a grown-up thing to do!

"Oh, yes," I say.

So Madame Marie shows me how to guide my needle

in and out,

in and out,

through the holes in the button.

I do it over and over and over again.

Then she shows me how to make a loop

and slip the needle through.

The knot pulls tight.

The button won't fall off.

"Well done," says Madame Marie.

Her praise is rare.

I know I have done a good job.
I sew on four more buttons
before Mama comes through the door that evening,
Madame Marie shows her what I have learned.
"My, these are strong!" Mama says,
testing the buttons.
"I couldn't do a better job myself."

Mama hums a tune she likes
as we climb up the stairs to our apartment.
She does that when she's happy.
She forgets to ask about my day at school.
I decide I'll never, *ever* skip school again!

~ A Second Secret ~

One day, Madame Marie asks me to come into her kitchen.
Together, we fill a box with food to send to Papa.
Now that he is a prisoner in Germany, not France,
we don't get many letters from him.
"I registered myself as *his* godmother too,"
Madame Marie tells me.
"That way I can send him packages,
just like your mama does."
She fits cans of beans and meat together.
I drop in some candies I have saved,
wrapped in red and gold.
Madame Marie covers the box with paper
and winds string around it . . .
once, twice, three times.
I put my finger on the string for her so she can tie it tight.

"Is Germany far away?" I ask her.

"Very far," she says.

"Will Papa come home one day?"

"But of course!" she says. "I'll tell you a secret.

When your papa left for the army,
I made a yellow blanket for him, just like yours.
I stitched a holy medal on it,
one of Saint George, the dragon slayer.
He's the patron saint of soldiers.
I told your papa that whatever happens,
he must hold on to that blanket.
He promised me that he would bring it back home.
So don't worry.
Your father will keep his promise."

What a good secret!
Saint George is looking after Papa.
They have the same name.
My blanket has kept me safe so far.
Maybe Papa's blanket will work for him too.

~ My Orange ~

Our teacher hangs a photograph of Marshal Pétain on the wall.
"He's the good father of France," she tells us.
"He makes sure every French schoolchild eats lunch."

Lentil soup.
Boiled rutabagas.
Kidney beans with lard.
These are what our good father gives us most days.
But tomorrow, our teacher says, will be different.
Marshal Pétain will show special fatherly love to some.
Children like me, whose fathers are brave prisoners,
will get an orange!
All we have to do is show papers
proving our fathers are prisoners.
I haven't seen an orange in a long time.
I can't wait to tell Mama.

Mama isn't as excited as I am.
I can tell she doesn't like Marshal Pétain.
But the next day she takes me to get my orange anyway.
We have to climb up some stairs
and wait in line at an old building.
The crates of oranges are emptying fast.

At last, it's our turn.

Mama shows the papers that prove my father is a prisoner.

The lady puts a big round orange in my hand.

Mama kisses me good-bye

and rushes down the stairs to go to work.

I carry my bright orange carefully through the gray streets.

A crowd of neighbors has gathered at our *Métro* station.

Leah, the corner grocer's wife, is there.

She's smiling, holding hands with her little one-armed son, Noe.

A tall boy I know, Leon, is there too.

I wonder what the crowd is looking at.

I tug on Leon's shirt.

"Odette!" he says. "Want to see?"

I nod.

First, he takes off his cap and plops it on my head,

grinning at me.

Then he lifts me up onto his strong shoulders.

He holds my feet with his hands

so I won't fall.

I feel safe and happy with Leon.

A gypsy is showing off his trained goat.

The goat climbs a ladder, and stands
at the top, hooves shaking.
He can't finish his trick
until everyone puts something in the gypsy's hat.
I feel sorry for the goat, but all I have is my orange.
I'm *not* giving that up!
"Put me down," I whisper into Leon's ear.
"Please."
I give him back his cap and he winks at me.
It's time to head home.

I show my orange to Madame Marie.
"Oh, my!" she says. "How splendid.
Take it upstairs and share it with your mama after supper."
I put the orange in the middle of our oak table,
the one with the animal feet.
Then I open our shutters and look out at the square.
The girls from the convent school aren't there today.
Maybe they are in church praying to God the Father,
the one they say created the world in seven days.
They tell me he takes care of us.
I'm not sure about this.
He never gives us oranges like Marshal Pétain.

~ An Empty Bag ~

Mama's at the door,
holding a bag made of tied string.
Inside it I see onions and potatoes . . . and crumpled paper.
Just then, Madame Marie comes in from the courtyard.
"What did you find at the market today, Berthe?" she asks.
Mama shrinks.
She looks like a schoolgirl caught cheating
when she slowly opens her bag.
It's stuffed mostly with the newspaper.

"*Mon amie*," says Madame Marie, "I'm surprised at you!"
She takes the bag to her kitchen and brings it back.
Now it's filled with cheese, bread, and homemade jam.
"If you can't find food, you must ask me,"
Madame Marie tells my mother.

Mama nods.
We climb the stairs together.
As long as Madame Marie is around,
we are not allowed to go hungry.

～ Mama's Story ～

At supper, I ask Mama if what
the convent girls have told me is true,
that there's a God the Father who cares for us?
"No," she says.

"Then who made the world?" I ask.
"Who was there at the very beginning?"

Mama says she will tell me the story if I finish my supper.
I pick up my fork and she begins.
"In the beginning was a beautiful meadow.
In the meadow was a cow, the Original Cow.
She had lots of milk.
Two babies, a boy and a girl, drank the cow's milk.
They grew up strong and healthy.
Then they married and had children.
Those children grew up and had more children.
Soon there were lots of people all over the world."

My plate is empty now.
It's time at last to eat my orange.
I peel it carefully and eat just one section.
Its juice fills my mouth with sharp sweetness.
I give a piece to Mama and think about the story she told me.

I'm pretty sure she made it up, just for fun.

Cows are nice, but I know they don't give you oranges.

God never gives them to us, either.

Not like our good father, Marshal Pétain.

~ Two More Secrets ~

Mama, like Papa, joins the fight for France.
She tells me her work is secret.
She gets money for guns to fight the enemy soldiers.
She helps find hiding places for children in trouble.
Sometimes visitors come.
I hear them whisper secret passwords at the door
before Mama will let them in.
"You must never tell anyone about our visitors,"
says Mama.
"If the wrong people find out, it will be the end of me."
I promise her I will never tell anyone.

Mama tells me another big secret.
She and her friends have made a plan
to keep their own children safe.
"You know the Nazis don't like Jews," she says.

Of course I do!
Jews are not allowed to own or use telephones.
We can't have bicycles, either.
What's next?
Will we be forbidden to play ball?
To jump rope?

Mama goes on.

"If it gets too dangerous in Paris, Odette,

you must go to a safe place in the country.

Cécile and Paulette and Suzanne will go with you on the train."

I like these girls.

They are friends of my family.

A train trip sounds like fun too.

But I could never go away and leave my mother!

"I want to stay here with you, Mama," I say.

"I don't care if it's dangerous."

"For now you will," says Mama.

She strokes my hair.

"For now, we will be together.

But we have a secret hiding place planned for you.

Just in case."

Mama tells me how I will get to the country . . .

a lady she trusts will take me.

I hope "just in case" never comes.

My father is already gone.

I can't live without my mother!

～ The Raid ～

Am I dreaming?
It's the middle of the night.
But I hear a thunder of footsteps on our staircase.
A fury of knocks at our door.
I'm awake, but too frightened to move,
so I pretend to be asleep.
I listen in my bed while Mama stumbles to the door.
Soldiers burst in.
They say they are here to arrest Mama . . .
and Papa too!

"M-m-my husband is a prisoner of war," Mama stutters.
"Look," she says. "Here are his letters."
All the while, the men bang open
cupboards and drawers,
searching for who-knows-what?

Just then, another voice.
Madame Marie arrives at our door.
"For shame," she scolds the men,
"disturbing the home of a French soldier!
Don't you know the wives of prisoners
are to be left in peace?"

"Excuse us," says the leader.
"There has been a mistake.
Your letters, Madame."
He and his soldiers stomp out.

"Marie," says my mother, her voice still shaking,
"I have money and papers hidden here.
If they had found them. . . ."
She never finishes her sentence.

Madame Marie soothes Mama.
"But they did not," she says, "and they never will.
We'll find a better place to hide your papers.
Thank God the child slept through this all."

Soon, Madame Marie leaves and our front door closes.
Mama comes back into the room we share.
She touches my shoulder . . .
her hand is cold and trembles.
My heart pounds so hard I am afraid she might feel it
right through my nightgown.
But Madame Marie said it was good that I was asleep,
so I still pretend I am.

I hold Charlotte and keep my eyes shut.
At last Mama climbs back into her bed.
I lie awake for a long time in the dark.
I listen to the shuddery sound of her breath.

The soldiers didn't say anything about me.
If my father weren't a soldier,
would they have taken Mama away
and left me alone?
I don't know the answer to this question,
and I can't ask anyone.

"Wake up, Odette," Mama calls in the morning.
"Time for school."
She irons my dress as usual,
but her hands are still trembling,
just a little,
as she smooths it.
I put my dress on while it's still warm,
and eat the bread and jam on my plate.
I look for my homework, but it's not where I left it.
Mama finds it with Papa's letters.
I don't ask how it got mixed up with them.

Mama pins back her hair and puts on lipstick.
She locks the door when we leave.

We both pretend
it's just another day.

∾ Trouble ∾

Soldiers slap posters up on the walls of Paris.
All Jews, aged six and older,
must sew yellow stars on their clothes for everyone to see.
The only reason for this, it seems to me,
is to make it easy to find Jews
and make life even harder for them.

Mama and I go to the police station and get six stars . . .
three for her and three for me.
"Can you believe they made me *pay* for these?"
she asks my godmother.
Madame Marie shakes her head.
Mama shrugs.
What can we do?

Madame Marie checks the stitching on my star
before she sends me off to school the next day.
"Don't try to cover it up," she warns me.
"You could get into trouble for that!"

I creep along next to the buildings on my way to school.
My star is too bright.
It screams to everyone I pass,

"See this girl?
She's a Jew!"
I clutch my schoolbag close to me.
Suddenly, two huge soldiers loom on the sidewalk in front of me.
Without thinking, I cover my star with my schoolbag.
One soldier sees me.
He grabs my schoolbag,
tears it away,
and throws it on the pavement.

Will he beat me?
Kick me?
Take me away from Paris and my mother?
Things like this happen to Jews every day now in Paris.

"No!" I say. I put up my hands.
"No, please. . . ."

But this time the soldier and his friend just laugh.
Together they stagger away.

I can't move.
I just stand and stare after them.

When they lurch around the corner into the next street,
I slump down on the curb.
I sit there until my heart stops pounding.
When I can breathe again,
I stand up and walk to school.

But even at school it's not safe.
On the playground, children attack me.
They try to shove my face in the playground toilet.
A teacher comes to help.
After that, I stay close to her.
But still these children hiss at me:
"Coward! Teacher's pet! Jew!"
I hide inside during recess.

On the walls are pictures of country children in costume.
The ones I like best show children from Alsace and Brittany.
They have kind, soft faces.
Why can't I live there?
Those country children wouldn't beat me up, would they?

What about the other Jewish children at school?
Are bad things happening to them?

I don't know because I don't dare ask.

I'm afraid to tell Mama about what's happening at school too.

She has enough worries.

So I tell Charlotte, but I tell her to keep it a secret.

Charlotte is good at that, and so am I.

~ My Cousins ~

On Thursdays in Paris, children don't have to go to school.
That is the day I visit my cousins,
the ones who live near the Père Lachaise Cemetery.
Mama never says so,
but I know these cousins are poor.
They don't have a toilet in their apartment like we do.
All they have is a stinky room with a hole in the ground,
way down the hall from their apartment.
They have to share it with other families too.

One Thursday, I try to sneak down the narrow back streets
that lead to my cousins' apartment.
I stay away from the soldiers
who strut along the avenues.
But I do have to cross one big street.
I hold my breath
when I pass in front
of the motorcycles, cars, and trucks.
On the other side,
a soldier darts out of the bakery right in front of me,
eating an éclair.
I almost bump into him!
Startled, I jerk back for an instant,

then recover.

I try to look calm as I walk toward the Passage des Amandiers.

But inside, my heart still pounds.

Past the bakery, I enter that dim alley.

It smells like cooked cabbage and urine.

Babies scream, workers hammer, women yell.

No soldiers can be seen, but I'm still afraid.

Anything can happen in a neighborhood like this. . . .

but above the din,

I hear the sweet sound of my cousin Serge's violin.

I follow it to safety.

I'm always hungry to hear Serge's music!

We never listen to music at home.

Jews had to hand over their radios to the police,

but Mama hid ours in the closet.

We listen to it only for the BBC news.

Serge sees me across the courtyard, but he keeps on playing.

I don't want him to stop.

When I'm close enough, I sit down cross-legged at his feet.

I feel like a small frog before a secret prince.

I look up at Serge's deep-set eyes,
his delicate fingers holding his violin and bow.
The music makes everything else—
the dirty alley,
the shouts and screams—
fade slowly away.

When Serge is done,
he lifts the violin from his shoulder.
Seeing his bright yellow star jolts me back to here and now.
I touch my star to make sure it's where it's supposed to be.
Serge places his violin in its case,
closes the cover,
and clicks the latch shut.

I follow Serge into the two rooms
where his whole family lives and works.
The first room is the only one with a window.
That's where Uncle Motl and my big cousin Maurice work
on their noisy knitting machine.
Above it is a loft, where the younger children sleep.
The second room is where everyone
eats, washes, cooks, plays, reads, and gossips.

A long table fills the center,
with chairs around it and beds on the side.
At least one lamp glows there all the time.
Aunt Miriam's sweet-smelling onion soup
simmers on the stove.

Maurice lifts me up to see their calendar.
It has a joke printed on it for every day of the year.
"The waiter puts coffee on the man's table," Maurice reads.
'It looks like rain,' he says to his customer.
'Tastes like it too,' says the man."
Everyone laughs.
Fake wartime coffee is terrible.

My younger cousins beg to see tomorrow's joke.
"No," says Maurice. "Let's save it."

So Uncle Motl shares a joke with us.
"Did you know Hitler's dog has no nose?" he asks.

"No?" says Charles. "How does it smell?"

"Terrible," says Uncle Motl.

Maurice pinches his nose.
He pretends to march like a stick soldier.
Sarah, Charles, Serge, and I all fall in line behind him.
Around and around the table we go.
Aunt Miriam helps little Henriette
clap time for us.

The soldiers are scary,
the alley is dirty,
my cousins' apartment is dark and crowded.
But when we're together,
nothing can stop us from having fun.

Henriette Melczak, almost three years old

~ Angels and Demons ~

One Thursday, my boy cousins aren't home.
Sarah whispers that they have gone swimming,
even though it's forbidden!

"Can you girls take Henriette for a walk?"
Aunt Miriam asks Sarah and me.
But where can we go?
Parks, cafés, and museums are forbidden to Jews too.
So we just wander along the main street.
We look in all the shop windows.

"Let's play a game," says Sarah.
"We can each choose one thing from every window . . .
but *only* one!"
We've played this game before.
It's like shopping but without money.

Our favorite place is the chandelier shop.
So many shiny lights,
glittering with diamonds!
Henriette wants them all.
"Don't be silly, Henriette," says Sarah.
"How could we fit all those lamps over one table?"

When we reach the doll hospital,
Henriette studies ladies, babies, clowns, and sailor dolls.
Then she frowns.
"What if you don't come back right away for your doll?
Will the doll doctor give it to someone else?"

"Never," says Sarah.
"The doctor knows everyone must have her own doll."
Henriette nods.
But soon she grows thirsty and begins to whine.
We go to a café and ask for water.

The barman stares at our stars and says nothing.
Sarah puts money on the bar.
"I don't sell water," says the barman.
"Go away. I can't serve you."
Henriette starts to cry.
We don't know what to do.
We know Jews must never make a fuss.

When we pass a small basement library,
Sarah thinks of a way to stop her sister's crying.
"Look," she says to me, "you and I are wearing the star.

But Henriette isn't.
If she were alone, they couldn't tell she's Jewish.
They'd let her in."

"You can't leave her alone!" I say.

"Of course not," says Sarah.
"Just watch, you'll see."

Henriette peers through the library window.
"You go down first, Henriette," says Sarah.
"The librarian will see you are alone and ask you questions.
Don't answer right away.
She'll try to make you feel good,
show you picture books.
Maybe she'll offer you a drink.
When she's busy with you, Odette and I will come down."

Clutching the handrail,
chubby little Henriette walks down to the library,
all by herself.
Sarah and I wait a few minutes,
then go down the steps into the library too.

The librarian spots our yellow stars.
She drops the book she's showing to Henriette.
Sarah picks it up and hands it to her.
"Are you her mother?" the librarian asks Sarah.
My cousin's big for thirteen.

"No," says Sarah, "I'm her sister.
I thought I lost her . . .
but I know how much she loves books.
I thought she might be here.
And she is!"

Henriette gazes up at her big sister like an innocent angel.
"Sarah, will you read to me?" she asks.
"Please?"
The librarian's eyes dart around quickly.
No one has seen us, or our yellow stars.

"All right," she says.
She flutters her hands
toward the picture-book corner.
"Take the children over there and stay there.
I'll be at my desk."

"You're so kind," says Sarah.

Open books cover our stars like shields.
Henriette forgets she is thirsty.
The librarian, our gatekeeper,
pretends we are children like any others.
All afternoon, we read fairy tales.
In our cave of bookshelves,
we feel safe from the evil giants
marching down the street.

∾ Lies ∾

Someone's crying.
The sound of it pulls me from my dreams.
I open my eyes.
It's still dark.
I go to the window and push open one shutter,
just a crack.
I look down and see little one-armed Noe.
His mother, Leah, helps him put on his jacket.

Rumpled people are being herded down the street.
They all carry bags and bundles.
A bearded man stumbles and a policeman pushes him along.
All the people are "yellow star" people.
All of them are Jews like me.

Madame Marie bursts in.
She wakes Mama by pulling the blankets off her bed.
"Hurry!" she says.
"The police are coming . . . they're filling trucks with Jews!"
Mama and I pull on our dresses as fast as we can.
Mama grabs a coat and shoes
and we fly down the spiral staircase.
Madame Marie pushes us into the broom closet

inside her small workroom.
She shuts the door just in time.
The doorbell rings.

Loud men trudge into the hallway.
"We're rounding up foreign Jews," they say.
"We're going to rid France of them forever."

"Wonderful!" says Madame Marie.
"Those Jews have taken our jobs and money for too long."
Then she offers them a drink . . .
to toast their courage, she says.

Frozen inside the dark closet,
Mama and I cannot see, but we can hear.
Madame Marie and the men are just outside the door.
If the door were open,
I could touch them.

Mama's fingers find my yellow star.
Silently, stitch by stitch, she begins to rip it off.
I listen hard.
I hear the sound of drinks being poured.

Glasses clink in a toast.

Chairs scrape around Madame Marie's table,

only a reach away from our hiding place.

The men boast and laugh.

Suddenly someone says to Madame Marie,

"Where are *your* Jews?"

His companions fall silent.

Our bodies stiffen.

Our breathing all but stops.

"Long gone!" says Madame Marie.

"They ran away to their country house.

Good riddance to them, I say."

More drinks are poured.

But then, stern words.

"You know, Madame, if you lie to us, you'll be sorry,"

one man warns her.

"We'll pack you into a truck along with them

and send you far away!"

My godmother sounds insulted.

"Me? Do I look like a friend of Jews?"

I'm confused . . .
how can she say such terrible things?
She *is* our friend . . . one of our *best* friends!

But suddenly, I know she's lying.
She's saying bad things about Jews to keep us safe.

The same voice, still stern,
"Just to be sure, we'll go up to their apartment."
Mama grabs my hand, squeezes it too tight.

But Madame Marie keeps the men away
from our just-slept-in sheets and blankets.
"Oh, you don't want to do that!" she says.
"You know how those foreign Jews are, filthy as pigs.
When they were living there,
I'd knock on their door only when I had to.
I'd say what I had to say quickly
and hold my breath as long as I could.
Then I'd run back down the stairs
as fast as my old legs would carry me.
Don't go up there if you don't have to.
Their apartment still stinks to high heaven.

Anyway, our bottle's nearly empty.
Why not help me finish it?"

We wait, cold bare toes pressed tight to the floor.
The smell of sour mops is all around.
My body shakes, hard.
But I don't make a single sound.

Finally, the loud men push their chairs
back in to the table.
"*Merci, Madame,*" they say.
"*Au revoir.*"

Heavy footsteps echo through the hallway.
The door slams.
Silence.
Madame Marie frees us from the closet.
"How can I thank you?" Mama asks Madame Marie.
She takes my godmother's hands in her own.

Madame Marie shrugs.
She needs her hands back to clear away the glasses.
"No time for that.

We must get Odette to the railway station
as we planned."

I look up at my mother.
"You'll come with me, won't you, Mama?" I ask.

∿ Torn in Two ∿

Mama's sad eyes turn to me.
"No, Odette," she says, "I must leave you now.
It's time for you to go to the country,
with our friends."
Mama's brown curls quiver just a little
as she tries to smile.
She takes me in her arms and rocks me back and forth.
Then she kisses my cheeks three times.
She wipes off my tears with her fingers in between.
With one last quick hug, she leans over
and begins to tie her shoes.

"Mama!" I scream.
I clutch her, hard.
"Don't go!"

Mama puts her finger to my lips.
"Shhh, Odette," she says.
She drops her coat, then kneels next to me.
We look at each other, face-to-face.
Mama's fingertips trace my cheeks, my ears.
"I must go now, right away, *chérie*," Mama says.
"Maybe I can warn your aunt and cousins about the trucks."

"Let me come with you!" I beg.
"I'll be good . . . I promise. Please!"
I feel like I'm being torn in two.

Mama's face twists away.
"No, Odette," she says. "That would be too dangerous.
You must go with our friends to a safe place, remember?
Cécile and Paulette and Suzanne
will be waiting for you at the train station.
You girls will all go together."

Mama stands up.
"Don't be sad, Odette," she says.
"It's only for a little while . . .
until we can be together again."
She blows me a kiss,
and she slips through the glass-topped door.
I watch her in the hallway.
She belts her coat tightly around her.
Then she opens the huge wooden door
and disappears into the street.

~ Courage ~

I look up at my godmother, trembling.
My heart pounds down in my stomach.
I know I have to go with Paulette and Cécile and Suzanne.
We have known each other all our lives.
Our mothers are friends.
But we are not together, not yet!
How can I go to the railway station all alone?

Madame Marie plucks away the last few threads
left on my dress from my star.
She smoothes the fabric with her fingertips.
Suddenly, I grab her and bury my face in her dress.
I cling to her and sob.
How can I leave my home,
my mother, my godmother too?
I won't do this!
I'll never be able to do this!

"*Courage, ma petite,*" Madame Marie says,
and pats my back.
"Don't worry.
I'll fetch Henri from work.
He'll take you on the *Métro* to the railway station."

I take a deep breath.
My heart rises back into my chest.
Monsieur Henri,
with his walrus mustache and his kind, droopy eyes,
is as big and strong as the mountains he comes from.
I know he'll protect me.

"Come now," says my godmother
as she wipes my face.
"I'll help you pack."
She tiptoes into the hallway and listens.
No one is coming downstairs.
Together we creep up to my apartment.
Madame Marie closes the door,
then the bedroom shutters.

The school year has just ended.
My godmother takes
my notebooks and pencils out of my schoolbag.
She puts in clean underwear,
the blue sweater my mother knitted,
a print dress she made for me.
I bring her my doll.

"Ah, no, my little rabbit.
Charlotte cannot go in this bag."

"I have to bring Charlotte!" I say.
Panic rises into my chest . . .
I can't go without my doll!

"No," says Madame Marie, her mind made up.
"You can take only a small bag.
A big one might attract attention,
and Charlotte cannot fit in here."
She puts a finger to her lips
to tell me to be quiet.
"You and Charlotte say good-bye for now.
Then come downstairs.
I'll have your breakfast waiting."

My godmother slips out the door.
I take Charlotte and go to my mother's bed.
I collapse onto her rumpled sheets,
soak in her smell.
Then I see the photograph of my father.
I can't take Charlotte, but Papa can go in my schoolbag.

I take out my blue sweater
and wrap it around his photograph.
"There!" I whisper to Charlotte.
I shove the sweater inside my schoolbag and buckle it.
"Now I'm ready to go."

I sit Charlotte down on my pillow and smooth her hair.
"You must be brave, *chérie.*
It's only for a little while."
I kiss her cheek.
I open the door and listen.
Silence.
Sunbeams stretch down from the skylight,
warming the hallway.
Even so, my spine prickles
as I tiptoe down the creaking stairs.

~ My Escape ~

Monsieur Henri takes my small hand in his large one.
He pushes open the heavy wooden door
leading into the rue d'Angoulême.
Two tall soldiers loom like giants
right outside our apartment building.
They're carrying guns.
Monsieur Henri's grip on my hand tightens.
Trucks still rumble along the street.
"Look at your feet," Monsieur Henri says softly,
when the soldiers are far enough away.
"If anyone calls your name, don't answer."

I can't breathe.
I can't think beyond my feet.
One step at a time, I push the pavement away.
It sticks to my feet.

In slow motion,
Monsieur Henri and I pass the convent,
the pharmacy, and the chain factory.
People leaf through their newspapers as always
at the Café de la Baleine.
Rolls of cheery oilcloth greet customers,

as they do every day,
at the hardware store.
The smell of fresh bread fills the morning air,
as it does every morning,
at the bakery.

But this is not *every* morning.
It's the most terrible morning of my life.

I clutch the big hand of Monsieur Henri.
I force my feet onward,
up the hill to the arched *Métro* station.
At the sight of it, the spell on my feet breaks.
I run for the stairs, away from the street,
into the safer darkness.
Monsieur Henri snatches me back.
"Don't rush," he whispers. "Act natural."

When the *Métro* train pulls into the station,
I head for the last car, the one for Jews.
But Monsieur Henri leads me to another.
We sit down side by side.
"What a fine, well-behaved granddaughter you have,"

says a gray-haired woman.

Her black-feathered hat frightens me.

Monsieur Henri, my new grandfather, nods at her silently.

I am frozen.

I sit like a statue.

I stare straight ahead.

When the *Métro* train pulls into the big railway station,
the Gare du Nord,

Monsieur Henri takes my hand in his.

He steers me out the sliding doors.

The big station is full of people, all in a rush.

Will Paulette, Cécile, and Suzanne be there?

Yes, three little Jewish girls in starless summer dresses
wait under the big clock, just as we planned.

A lady holds the hand of the littlest one.

"*Au revoir, ma petite*," Monsieur Henri says to me.

"*Au revoir, Monsieur Henri*," I reply.

I swallow hard.

He's leaving me now.

Don't cry, Odette.
Stay calm, his eyes tell me.
But his voice says,
"Mind this lady.
And obey the mama and papa in your country family."
Then Monsieur Henri pats me on the head
and disappears into the crowd.

Holding hands, the other little girls and I
climb up onto the train.
Paulette and Cécile are big girls, like me.
Suzanne is the smallest of our group, only two.
We wait and wait for the train to leave.
We watch other travelers say good-bye
to their loved ones.
No one says good-bye to us.
Suzanne, Cécile, Paulette, and I try not to cry.
But when at last the locomotive pulls out of the station
and the whistle wails mournfully,
little Suzanne does too.
The lady we are with puts an arm around her.

"Where are we going?" I ask the lady.

"To the Vendée," she tells me.
I've never heard of this place.

"Is it far away?" I ask.
"How long will it take to get there?"

The lady glances around her.
Is anyone listening?
"No more questions," she whispers.
"If the conductor comes, pretend you are asleep."

I close my eyes.
The train rumbles along through endless suburbs.
We are leaving all we know behind.
How long will this go on?
Everything has changed since the war came.

A voice in my head repeats words I have heard,
"One thousand years of the Third Reich."
Hitler and his mean soldiers are the Third Reich.
But what does "one thousand years" mean?
Someone once tried to explain it to me like this:
Imagine a person lives the longest possible life, a hundred years.

At the end of that time he has a grandchild,
and that grandchild lives a hundred years.
If that happens ten times over,
a thousand years will have gone by.

I'll never see the end of the Third Reich.
My parents, Madame Marie and Monsieur Henri,
and my cousins won't, either.
My friends and I will just ride and ride into a gray, dark tunnel.
We'll never escape, not ever.

∾ Soup, a Swing, and Another Secret ∾

Our stomachs growl, louder and louder.
We've been on the train for hours,
with only a little bread and cheese to share.
But at last my friends and I arrive in Chavagnes-en-Paillers,
our new village in the Vendée.
Small houses encircle the church like a fallen halo.
The lady who came with us on the train
tells us we're going to live in one of these houses,
with a blacksmith's family.
We knock on a door.

A small woman lets us in.
She looks young, like a mother.
But she carries a cane like a grandmother.
Tap! Tap! Tap!
She takes us into her kitchen.
A pot of soup steams on the black iron stove.
I glance at it hopefully, but the woman says nothing.
A real grandmother knits nearby.
Tap! Tap! Tap!
The younger woman takes us into the garden,
to see pigeons in a dovecote.
A swing dangles beside it.

But then we march back across the kitchen,
past the steaming soup,
and up the stairs to a small bedroom.
The woman ushers us all inside and closes the door.
Even though it's summer, I feel cold.
Is it because I'm so hungry?
I sit on my fingers to keep them warm.
At last the woman speaks.

"Listen carefully, children," she says.
"I'm Madame Raffin.
I'm going to take care of you.
If you do everything I tell you to do,
you can eat the soup and play with the pigeons.
First of all, never, ever say that you are Jewish, *no matter what*!
I'm going to teach you to make the sign of the cross.
When you can do that and say two longer prayers by heart,
I will open the door."

The sign of the cross?
What's that?
Madame Raffin touches her forehead, her heart,
and each shoulder,

"In the name of the Father, the Son, and the Holy Spirit,"
she says.
We copy her.
Is this praying?
I've never prayed before.

Madame shows us how to kneel and put our hands together
with our fingers pointing up.
"Our Father, who art in heaven," we say after her,
the whole prayer, over and over.
Then, "Hail Mary, full of grace," again and again.
I'm not sure what these words mean.
Madame Raffin says that's not important, not right now.
We just need to remember these words.
That way people will think we're Christians.

At last Madame Raffin is satisfied
that we know the prayers by heart,
that we won't make a mistake.
She takes our hands and squeezes them for courage.
"Never forget that you are Christians," she says.
"Your fathers are French soldiers taken prisoner.
Your mothers have jobs in Paris.

They sent you to live in my house
so that you'll be well fed and safe."
We promise.
I know it will be easy for me.
I am used to keeping secrets.
Madame Raffin opens the door.

Mmm . . . soup.

Odette and her foster family in Chavagnes-en-Paillers.
Clockwise, from top left: Cécile Popowicz, Jacques
Raffin, Paulette Klaper, Suzanne Klaper, Jean Raffin,
and Odette, 1942

～ A New Life ～

For the rest of July and all of August,
we listen hard and speak little.
We watch everything.
We learn how to act
just like all the other village children.

Two brothers belong to our new family.
Jacques and Jean are the Raffins' sons and our teachers.
At first, Cécile, Paulette, Suzanne, and I feel shy with them.
But the boys aren't shy.
They show us how to hold the pigeons.
They tell us scary stories
about a ghost who lives at the bottom of the well.
We play hide-and-seek together in the garden.
They tease us and teach us riddles.
I've never had brothers and sisters before . . . it's fun.

Madame Raffin asks us to pick green beans and tomatoes.
All summer long we twist vegetables from their stems.
She takes us mushroom picking in the forest too.
Sometimes Monsieur Raffin takes us fishing.
He teaches us the names of all the glittering fish
we scoop up in his net.

We have so many good things to eat,
I almost forget
what it felt like to be hungry in Paris,
to sleep with my fists screwed up tight under my stomach
to make it feel full.

We don't have many toys,
but the grandfather of our house carves us whistles from reeds.
He shows us how to make toy pots and pans from acorns too.
Best of all,
we can go anywhere we like in our new village.
We can do anything anyone else can do.
No one knows that we're Jews.
I climb trees
and walk along the tops of stone fences.
If I fall and tear my dress,
the grandmother in my new family mends it for me.
She would never think of sewing a yellow star on my dress.
I wonder if she's ever even seen one.

Monsieur and Madame Raffin,
Jacques, Jean, and the grandparents,
Cécile, Paulette, and Suzanne . . .
these are the people in my new family.

When September comes,
Madame Raffin takes Cécile, Paulette, and me to school.
Suzanne wants to come too, but she is only two.
All the big girls in the village go to the convent school,
Madame Raffin explains.
"These children have been in a bombing,"
she tells the nun in charge.
"They may act strangely for a while.
Take no notice."
But no one seems to think we act strangely.
By now, we behave just like all the other village children.

Someday I'll tell Mama that she was right,
that I do feel safe here with my new family in the Vendée.
I wonder what she would say
if she knew that once in a while,
when I swing in the garden and look up at the sky,
I almost forget who I really am. . . .

*The photograph of Odette's father
that she kept throughout the war*

∾ Twilight ∾

Children in the Vendée go to bed at twilight.
Twilight is not day or night.
It is the time between.

Cécile and I share one small room and a bed.
Every night Madame Raffin kisses us good night.
As soon as she closes the door,
Cécile and I go to the open window.
Cécile always sits on the left. I always sit on the right.
"Look," Cécile says, gazing outside.
The sky is turning a deeper and deeper blue.
"Everything is so beautiful. And we're alive."
We thank God for our day.
"Tonight," Cécile always says,
"a bomb could fall and we could die.
Let's say good-bye to our parents."

So far I have not heard of any bombs falling in the Vendée,
but Cécile cannot forget the ones in Paris.
To make her feel better,
I go along with what Cécile tells me to do.
I imagine my mother's face.
It floats in the air just outside my window.

I tell her everything I have done that day, even the bad things.
I ask her to forgive me.
She does.

Then it's my father's turn.
My father's face is always the one in the photograph
Madame Raffin put on our mantelpiece.
Papa never smiles.
I can't feel his rough cheek or hear his voice.
I can't see the brown or shine of his eyes.
He is barely real to me anymore.
Still, he *is* my father, so I talk to him.
When I am done, Cécile takes her turn.

While she talks to her parents,
I study the stone wall across from us.
In the fading light it looks safe and strong,
like the wall of a fort.
When Cécile's parents have vanished
from outside our window,
Cécile closes the shutter.
Night enters our room.
We hug each other and say,

"If we die tonight, may we meet in heaven tomorrow."
At last we climb into bed.
Cécile goes first, against the wall.
Then me, on the outside.
Time to sleep.

Sometimes when I open my eyes in the morning,
I'm not sure where I am.
In heaven already, maybe?
I make up a way to check.
If the chest of drawers is still across the room,
then I know I am in Chavagnes-en-Paillers, my new village.
No one knows what it's like in heaven,
but I'm pretty sure there are no chests of drawers there.

~ Heaven ~

Every day in Chavagnes-en-Paillers brings new wonders.
I love to listen to Bible stories
and *The Lives of the Saints* at my school.
Our teachers tell us these stories are about real people,
good people who lived in other places and times,
not fairy-tale people.
Now all these real people are in heaven with God.
I hope I will meet them one day in heaven,
especially Saint Bernadette and Saint Terèse,
who are French like me.
But one day I learn that because I'm not baptized,
I can't go to heaven.
How can that be?
I want to go to heaven too!

I run to the church to pray.
The quiet and peace there,
the smell of beeswax,
the flickering candles,
the light that shines through the colored windows . . .
all these things calm me.
Sometimes, alone with God in church,
I can talk to Him.

I tell God everything.

I thank Him for bringing me to the Vendée.

I tell Him I miss my mother, Madame Marie, and my cousins.

But I make sure He knows I don't want to go back to Paris.

I'm just too afraid.

Then I ask God if I can go to heaven someday too.

One day when I'm at church an answer comes.

A peasant woman comes in.

She kneels in front of the altar of the Virgin Mary,

the mother of Jesus.

She talks to Mary out loud,

the way I talk to God in my heart.

She calls her "Madame Marie."

Ah, so Mary has the same name as my godmother!

It's my godmother's job to protect me—she already has.

She knows so many things.

I'm sure she'll know how to fix things with Mary,

and Mary will fix things with God.

That way I'll be able to go to heaven too.

~ Far Away ~

Life seems so safe in the country.
But I know it isn't, not really.
Many people in the Vendée are afraid of Jews.
They think Jews bring trouble.
If they knew who we *really* were,
they might tell the enemy soldiers about us.
That's why we have to pretend to be Christians.

Mama, my half-remembered Papa,
Madame Marie, and Monsieur Henri, . . .
they are all so far away.
I try to remember our square.
I can barely see the face of *The Thinker*
or hear the splash of the fountain.
I know Sophie's hiding in the country,
but I don't know what happened to Sarah and Henriette,
to Charles, Serge, and Maurice.
Maybe they've gone away too.
Paris seems only a faraway word,
light as a goose feather.

Still, Madame Raffin makes us write letters there every week.
I always write the same thing to my mother:

I am in good health. I hope you are too.
Everyone here is nice. I do my homework.
If you come to visit, please bring Charlotte.

One day Madame Raffin tells me
my mother will come at Christmas . . .
I can't wait to see her and my doll!

But what if she wants to take me back to Paris?
I don't want to go!
The children here all play with me.
I have new brothers and sisters.
We always have as much good food to eat as we want,
and I can walk to school with my friends.
We can go anywhere we want.
We can explore the village
and the woods and streams
all by ourselves!
I know the reason I feel safe in the country.
It's because *here*,
I am not a Jew.

In Paris, I am a Jew.

I do want to see Mama,

but I don't want to go back to Paris.

I don't want to hide from bombs and scary soldiers.

I don't want to wear a yellow star

and be attacked at school.

I don't want to be afraid

all the time,

nearly every single minute.

I don't want to live like that *ever* again!

∾ Mama Comes ∾

I count the days in December, and Mama comes at last.
Jews aren't allowed to travel, so she took off her yellow star.
The train was crowded with Christmas travelers.
No one stopped her to find out if she was Jewish.
My mother's coat,
the smell of her hair and her cologne,
her arms around me . . .
these things make everything else around me disappear.

I want to show Mama my new village.
"Not yet," she says.
"First I must talk to the Raffin family.
Go outside and play for a while."

"But Mama, did you bring Charlotte?" I ask.
She opens her small suitcase and out comes my doll.
She still wears the very dress knitted by Mama's hands,
and the apron I made with my godmother.
I hug Charlotte.
How I have missed her!
I take her outside on the swing.
Together we fly high into the sky.
At last, Mama comes out of the house.

She's looping her silk scarf around her neck,
her chin high, her face shining.
Now I remember, that's how she looks when she is happy!

At last it's time to take Mama to see what I love most . . .
the Christmas crèche in the church.
"Look, here's the Baby Jesus and his mother and father
and the ox and donkey.
The animals breathe on the baby to keep him warm."
The statues are almost as big as real people.
Mary gazes with loving eyes at her baby.
He holds out his arms and smiles at all the world.
I wish I could pick him up and hug him,
kiss his fat pink cheeks.

But Mama looks at it all, then looks away.
I've made a terrible mistake!
How could I forget she doesn't like things like this?
She can't get out of the church
and down the steps fast enough.
When we're back on the street,
Mama breathes a sigh of relief.
"It's so dark and musty in there!" she says.

"It's like an old lady's room,
crowded with knickknacks."

Mama likes the bakery better.
She can't take her eyes off the giant brioche.
"White bread is impossible to get in Paris," she says.
I show her the window of the general store too.
"Look at the wool!" Mama says. "So many colors!"

I remember the game I used to play in Paris with Sarah.
If I had my choice of one thing from the general-store window,
would I pick the wool for my mother to knit?
My eyes move to a silver rosary with pearl beads.
It's so beautiful.
Maybe I'd pick that.
I study them both.
Suddenly, I feel my mother's eyes on me.
"Let's move along now, Odette," she says.
She steers me away from the shop window.

Oh, dear, I've done it again!
There must be something I can show Mama that she'll like.
I know, I'll take Mama to my school.

Creeks crisscross through snowy meadows.
Here and there is a small farm
with smoke trailing from the chimney.
"It's so beautiful!" Mama says.

But when we arrive at the school, she won't go past the gate.
All I can show her is the cross
and the pretty statue of the
Virgin Mary outside.
"I don't understand all this fuss over crosses and statues,"
she says.
"But one day, if I come here to live,
I suppose you must teach me everything.
No one must guess that I'm not a Christian."

Mama?
Here?
Could she really come here and stay?
I know all the saints and holy days,
and when to stand and sit and kneel in church.
I know every single prayer by heart too.
If she comes, I'll teach Mama everything.

~ Country Ways ~

On the way back from the school,
I name all the trees I've climbed with Jean and Jacques.
I name all the fish I've caught with Monsieur Raffin,
all the mushrooms I've picked with Madame Raffin.
"I even know which ones are poisonous," I tell her.

Mama is happy that I know these things.
She has lots of questions.
"What do you drink at dinner?"
"Apple cider," I tell her.
"Where do you get the water for cooking and washing?"
"From our garden well."
"What do you do for heat?"
"We use the fireplace in the kitchen. The stove too.
Grandmother Raffin opens the oven door
and puts her feet up on the stovetop when she's cold.
We heat bricks in the oven too.
At night, we put them in our beds to keep warm.
Warm feet are important here."
Mama says she thinks the villagers are clever.
"Oh, yes," I agree.
"When we have a fancy meal and dessert is served,
we clean our plates with a piece of bread.

Then we turn them upside down
and use the bottoms for dessert plates."

"I must try that for myself," says Mama.

"And you know what else the villagers do that's clever?" I say.
"If someone has a loose tooth,
they don't go to the dentist.
Oh, no!
Madame Raffin ties a long string around the tooth.
She ties the other end to the handle of the back door.
Then she slams the door shut.
One scream and the tooth is out."
Mama doesn't say if she'll try that herself.

I change the subject back to food.
Mama's always interested in that.
"The day after Christmas the pigs are slaughtered.
That's the day women gather to make sausages and hams.
They smoke the meat by the fireplace.
Then, the best part of all!
They take all the leftovers and cook them together.
They say it's delicious."

My mother looks at me, shocked.

Her parents were strict Jews.

They never touched pork.

To them, it was dirty.

"Well, well," Mama manages to say,

"*that* I would like to see."

"Ask Madame Raffin," I say.

"I'm sure she'll invite you."

By this time, we've walked back to the church.

A baptismal party comes down the steps.

The baby, crying in his godmother's arms,

wears a long white lace dress.

Someone tosses a handful of candy

from the open church.

All the children run for the candy.

I show my mother the blue candies I've gathered.

"See, it's a boy!"

Mama takes the candy away.

"You can't eat candy off the dirty ground," she says.

"You'll get sick."

Tears start to come,
but I blink them back as best I can.
Crying is for babies, isn't it?

"That's not fair!" I say.
"We always do it."
Mama softens.
She looks left and right.
Everyone has gone home.
We go inside the church
and she washes my candy
in the holy-water font.
Then she wipes it on her sleeve.
She baptizes my candy and gives it back to me.
Now it is purified, and I can eat it.

Christmas comes and goes, and with it my mother.
She takes the train back to Paris,
and she doesn't try to make me go with her.
She never even mentions it.

Mama made me a pair of mittens,
pale blue with white snowflakes.

It's cold on New Year's Day, so I wear them.
That's the day children visit all the houses in our village.
"Happy New Year, good health,
and paradise at the end of your days," we tell everyone.
In return, they give us coins and candy.
People say it's bad luck
if children don't visit you
on the first day of the year.
I say it's good luck
to be in a place
where children are so important.

I jingle my cold coins in one of my new mittens.
My candy melts in the other.
I'll use one of my coins to light a candle in church,
to thank God that I can stay in the Vendée.

~ Mama Comes Back ~

Before the snowdrops can push up
out of the frozen ground,
Mama's back.
She did her secret work as long as she could in Paris.
The police arrested her!
They caught her in the apartment
of some Jews who had gone into hiding.
Mama swallowed some secret papers
before the police could find them.
They let her go that time.
But now it's too dangerous for Mama to stay in Paris.
She can't risk being caught again.

Mama says she's decided to live with me in the country.
"Can we stay in Chavagnes-en-Paillers?" I ask.
"I don't want to leave my new family and friends behind."

"No," says Mama. "It's better to go somewhere else.
We have to make sure that no one knows we're Jewish.
To do that we'll need a new last name.
What do you think? Grand or Petit?"

"Petit!" I answer. "And what will my first name be?"

"You don't need to change your name," Mama says.
"It's very French."
But she says she will change hers to Marie.

"Like Madame Marie," I say,
"and Madame Raffin."
And the Virgin Mary, I think,
but I don't say that out loud.

"Yes," says Mama, "like those two good women.
"Marie is also the French way of saying Miriam."

Where *is* Aunt Miriam? I want to ask.
Are Sarah, Charles, Henriette, Serge, and Maurice with her?
But somehow I know better than to ask.
Aunt Miriam and my cousins have gone away,
that much I know,
like lots of Jewish people.
But no one talks about the people who have gone away.
Doesn't anyone know what has happened to them?
Maybe it's better not to know.

~ A Small Stone Cottage ~

Too soon it's time to say good-bye to all the Raffins,
and to Cécile, Paulette, and Suzanne.
I hug them all, one by one.
As always, I try not to cry.
I remind myself that changes can be good.
Wasn't it good to come to the country from Paris?
Besides, now Mama and I are *together* again.
She says we'll see our friends again after the war,
when it's safe.
So the war won't last a thousand years after all.

Madame Raffin finds a small stone cottage for us to rent.
It's in her parents' village of La Basse Clavelière.
This village is only a few miles away,
but it takes two hours to walk there.
The path is narrow.
It winds over rocky hillsides.

Mama goes there first.
She cleans the cottage and makes it cozy for us.
When everything is ready, she comes back for me.
I have all my treasures packed:
my rosary and the holy pictures I have begun to collect.

There's one of the Virgin Mary in her blue dress,
one of the gentle Saint Joseph with his carpentry tools,
one of Saint Francis speaking to birds.

I also bring the photograph of my father in his soldier's uniform,
but Mama hides it in the linen closet.
Madame Marie will still send us his letters,
but now we must keep him a secret.
He wasn't a secret in my old village,
but here he will be.

"Don't talk about him," Mama warns me.
"Not ever!
Here we are Marie and Odette Petit.
Papa's name is foreign.
The peasants might wonder about that.
Let's not talk about Paris, either,
or even Chavagnes-en-Paillers.
We'll just talk about life here.
And we'll copy everything everyone else does in the village.
We want our neighbors to like us."
I don't tell her that by now,
I've almost forgotten about Papa, anyway.

The truth is,
I won't miss seeing his photograph,
not that much.

Frost coats the windows of our new cottage.
I draw pictures in it of what I've left behind:
my friends, our swing, the pigeons.
Mama builds a stove out of an old pail and some pipes.
She buys me wooden shoes called *sabots* with felt liners.
I can walk through mud in them and my feet stay dry.
When I get home, I leave my *sabots* at the door.
I wear my clean felt liners inside.

Two things frighten me at our new home.
One is the toilet . . . it's outside.
A terrible toilet,
a dark hole dug deep into the earth.
Now I know we are really poor,
maybe even poorer than my cousins used to be.
It's the worst toilet I've ever seen.
My mother says it's just part of peasant life,
and I will get used to it.
She's right. I do.

But the worst problem comes at night.
At the top of our cottage is an attic
with an old spinning wheel.
After dark, I hear spooky sounds.
I'm sure there's a ghost up there, spinning away.
Mama says no, it's only mice skittering around.
Still, I can't sleep.
I just can't help it,
I break down and cry in my bed.
I try to do it so that Mama can't hear me.
But she does hear me, night after night.
Finally, she gets me what I've always wanted . . .
a cat, to scare the mice away!
I call her Bijou.
She has spots and long white whiskers . . .
she's the cat of my dreams.
We play "Catch the String" for hours.

During the long winter evenings,
chestnuts roast in the fireplace.
Cabbage-and-onion soup simmers
in the big black pot over the fire.
Potatoes bake in the embers.

Mama reads by the fire.
The last sounds I hear before sleep
are now just the tiny footsteps of mice.
The ghost has disappeared,
but a few mice are still dancing in the attic.
Bijou sits on my feet and purrs.

～ True Peasants ～

The back of our house faces the center of our tiny village,
the place where everyone gathers to gossip
and to fetch water from the well.
Mama and I begin to meet people there.
The peasants speak *patois*, a kind of country French.
It's different from the French that people speak in Paris,
or even in Chavagnes-en-Paillers.
But I listen carefully and copy what people say.
Soon I can speak *patois* too.

I walk to school with the other children.
Our school is in the town of Saint-Fulgent.
It's a long way there, past the cemetery.
If an oxcart passes by,
a brave child might hang on to the back and hitch a ride.
The rest of us trudge along together, singing folk songs.
Our church is in Saint-Fulgent too.
Mama and I go there every Sunday.
So does everyone else from the nearby villages.
Mama doesn't know all the prayers yet.
When she's not sure of the words,
I tell her to close her eyes and pretend she's whispering them.
After Mass, the plaza in front of the church is like a fairground.
It's full of people who chat, picnic, flirt, and play.

The children in Saint-Fulgent go to school all year long—
but not the children in La Basse Clavelière.
No one seems to care what we learn.
When springtime comes, we stop going to school.
It's time to help with farmwork.
Except for one boy, Marcel,
who's been sick for a long time,
every child has to help.
Girls watch cows, weed and water, or peel potatoes.
Boys cure tobacco leaves, sow and plow, or mend tools.
All the children bring animals home at the end of the day.
It doesn't matter whose family you belong to.
If you're a child, you must help anyone who needs you.

When we have enough time,
my favorite place to play is in the forest.
I like to pretend I'm Joan of Arc, fighting for France.
Sometimes we dare each other
to climb to the tops of the highest trees.
We rob birds' nests of their eggs and eat them raw.
The older children teach the younger ones
which snakes are safe
and which ones can kill you.

It's important too to know which spiderwebs not to break.
Bad luck can come from breaking a Thread of Mary,
an almost-invisible straight web,
strong as a rope.

On busier days, we play in the village center.
I learn new games with sticks and stones.
Simone, who lives two doors away, becomes my best friend.
She likes my curly brown hair, and I like her wavy red hair.
She doesn't have her own doll . . .
but she does have four younger brothers.
Sometimes I let Simone hold Charlotte.
But most of the time, we help grown-ups work.

One day, a farmer lets me cut hay with a sickle,
far up in the hills,
all alone.
I work all morning in the heat, cutting grass for animals to eat.
At noon, the church bells ring out bright and clear.
It's time to say a noontime prayer, the Angelus.
Then I eat the food my mother packed for me
and work some more.
When I'm done, I'm tired but proud.

I've worked a whole field all by myself.
I've proved myself a true peasant child.

Mama is quick to learn country ways too.
She watches the peasants make soap and vinegar.
Then she tries it herself.
She learns which mushrooms are poisonous,
and which wild herbs to pick for salads.
She tears apart worn-out sweaters
and uses the yarn to make beautiful baby clothes.
Everyone admires her for this.

One day someone gives her half a pig
for helping with farmwork.
She makes ham, bacon, and pâté from it.
She takes the pig's intestine and washes it in the river.
Then she uses it for sausage casing.
My Parisian mama now seems just like a real peasant,
except in one important way.

I still have to watch over Mama in church.
I poke her so that she knows when to stand and kneel,
and when to say, "Lord, have mercy," and "Grant us peace."

"Watch now, you do it this way," I say.
I have to show her how to make the sign of the cross,
over and over again.

Mama, who is so good at so many things, is clumsy at prayer.
She's grateful when I help her, though.
"You must never, ever tell anyone our real name
or that we are Jewish," Mama says.
"This is a matter of life and death.
But I trust you.
I know that you can keep secrets."

She's right.
I'm an expert now at keeping secrets.

~ Signs ~

One day, dogs bark to tell us that Nazis have arrived
to camp in a nearby meadow.
My friend Simone and I run to see.
The soldiers came in big silver trailers.
We watch them unload . . .
beds and tables that unfold,
shiny lanterns and stoves.
The soldiers have boxes and boxes of food.
They offer us candy.
"Don't take it!" adults have always warned us.
"It might be poison."
But Simone and I take the sweets anyway.
We almost never get candy,
so we are willing to take a chance on being poisoned.
I hide my candy from my mother
and eat it alone.

Anyway, I think people here worry too much
about poisons, curses, and sickness.
They protect themselves with herbs and leeches.
Leeches are slimy worms.
The villagers use them to suck out bad blood.
The peasants also think that Jews bring bad luck.
I try not to think about that.

What would happen to us if they found out
Mama and I are Jews?
Maybe if I do more good deeds
the saints will be on my side.
God will send me a sign that everything will be all right.

What happens next
does not seem like a good sign.
Kittens are born in our village.
Five are homeless. No one will adopt them.
By tradition, children take the unwanted ones to Père René,
the oldest man in our village.
He has the biggest ears I've ever seen.
Does this mean he can hear better than anyone?

Père René throws the kittens into a black pond,
one by one,
with his six-fingered hand.

The tiny kittens struggle.
"Just look at them!
Not even a day old and they think they can swim."
The children who watch him laugh.
I feel a dull pain in my chest.

"Ah, so you're scared, little ones?"

Père René says to the kittens.

"Won't be long now."

A big boy named Paul throws stones at them.

One by one,

the kittens go under.

Soon the black pond is still.

"Time for my nap," says Père René,

and with a yawn and a stretch,

he leaves.

The children go off to play.

Everyone else accepts that these animals must die.

It's the way of the peasant world.

But me, I go back into my house

and hug Bijou

until she scratches her way out of my arms.

However, before long a good sign comes.

Mama wants to mail a package to Madame Marie.

She sends my godmother food when she can.

The post office is in Saint-Fulgent.

So my mother and I take the long walk there together.

I go to school that afternoon while

she goes to the post office
and buys things she needs.

That day, our teachers take us into a field to look at the clouds.
"What do you see?" the nuns ask.
"Oh, a bear!" a little girl says.
"No, it's a furry dog," another one says.
But I see a sewing machine!
Seated at it is Madame Marie.
I know she's there to protect my mother and me.
This is the sign I've been watching for!

When the school bell rings,
Mama's waiting for me.
She has two straw baskets.
One is full.
Inside is lamp oil, flypaper, new knitting needles,
and a loaf of fresh bread.
The other one is almost empty
except for a few cabbage leaves.
Mama gives the empty one to me to carry.
We walk along the quiet, dusty road back to our village.
An oxcart trundles by.

When it passes,
I follow Mama into a field of rutabagas.
She shows me how to pull them up.
I take one here, one from a few feet away.
Mama tells me to hide them in my basket under the leaves.

I know I'm stealing, but my mother told me to do it.
We need vegetables, and there are so many here.
Surely it won't matter if we take just a few?
Soon we are back on the road and all seems well.
Madame Marie will get a package of good country food:
meat, sausages, and pâté.
Mama has her new knitting needles
and fresh bread from town.
I carry the stolen rutabagas but also a wonderful secret . . .
the most powerful of all good omens.

Madame Marie has appeared in the sky.
We are safe.

∾ Accused ∾

When the fruit trees blossom pink,
it's time to build a village shrine to the Virgin Mary.
Père René, the old man who drowned the kittens,
divides his barn in two.
He puts his cows on one side.
On the other side, a statue of Mary moves in.
She wears her light blue robe and her golden crown.
All during the month of May,
people visit her and bring flowers.

One May morning,
I walk to school with other children.
A meadow shines with silver.
We've heard pilots sometimes drop tinsel over fields at night.
Are these shell casings?
No one seems to know for sure.
Could the shiny paper have chocolates inside?
We have to go see!

No, there's no chocolate, but the silver paper is so pretty.
We toss handfuls of it into the air
and watch them shimmer down.
One boy collects a huge pile of silver papers.

He sits down under a tree to count them.
The rest of us just grab as many as we can.
Someone says,
"Let's decorate the Holy Virgin's shrine!"
We run back to the village with our treasure.

Patient as ever,
Mary lets us decorate her with tinsel.
It shines on the white tablecloth in front of her,
and on the bouquets of rosebuds
in their milk cans and jars.
The cows are out for the day,
but their smell lingers with that of the roses.
A sheepdog comes in to see what's happening.
"Old Père René's dog!" someone whispers.
"Let's get out of here."

But before we can escape,
the wrinkled old man blocks the barn door.
He shakes his six-fingered hand at us.
"Not in school?
Not in the fields?
The day's still young and there's plenty of work to do.

But do you help your parents?
No, you make a mess of the Virgin's shrine."

"We're decorating it for her," says the oldest, bravest girl.
"Look at the silver.
Ours will be the prettiest shrine in any village."

Père René shakes his head.
"Anything to get out of all the work God planned for us
from the day Adam left the Garden of Eden. Bah!"

At the village center, I meet my friend Simone.
She's playing hopscotch.
But when she sees me coming,
she drops her marker and walks away.
Why, I wonder?
I follow her.
At first she won't speak to me, but then she says,
"I can't play with you anymore.
People say you and your mother are really Jewish.
Are you hiding from the Germans?"
Silence.
"You are, aren't you?"

My mouth drops open,
but no words come out.
Who thinks we're Jewish?
How did they figure it out?
But I don't have time to think about this.
Not now.

I swallow hard and reply.
"Jewish?
How could I be Jewish?
Lots of Christians have left Paris since the war began.
We had no eggs, no meat, no milk, no butter!
We had to hide in bomb shelters at night.
It was awful.
We came here because it's quiet and peaceful,
and there's lots of good food."

"I *knew* those people were lying," says Simone.
"You're too nice to be Jewish."
She smiles at me.
"Come on," she says as she pulls my hand.
"Want to go see my new baby brother?
He's the ugliest one yet!"

I feel faint with relief.

For a moment, I can barely see . . .

everything looks blurry, as if we're under water.

I grab Simone's hand and let her pull me along,

blinking until my sight clears.

Who are the people who suspect us? I wonder.

Should I run and tell Mama right now?

No, I'll act normal, I decide.

I'll wait until tonight to tell Mama everything.

~ Attacked ~

Like all the houses in our village,
Simone's house has two rooms.
One has a fireplace and a big table,
and the other a huge carved bed.
Simone's thin mother rests in the bed with her sleeping baby.
"Look how blessed I am with all these fine children, Odette!
Simone can keep house and milk cows as well as I can.
I don't know what I'd do without her!
In fact, I need her today.
Can you take the cows to the pasture this afternoon?"

"Of course," I say, proud to be asked.
Simone packs ham and rye bread for me for lunch.
She puts it in a satchel with some cider.

"Now, Odette," says her mother.
"You know where the cows are, behind the house.
Take them to the stream.
You can keep your cider cool in the deep water there."

At the stream, the four cows are happy
with all the water, grass, and shade.
After I find a good place to put my cider,

I pick wildflowers for Mary's altar.

Then I take off my rubber sandals

and wade into the water to look for frogs.

But a sound behind me makes me jump—is it the cows?

No, it's the village children marching toward me.

One look tells me they're not here to play.

They look like farmers ready to chop down a big tree.

Paul, the big boy who threw stones at the kittens, is the leader.

He has no family.

The old lady he lives with works him too hard,

almost as hard as a grown man.

Simone walks beside him.

I thought she had to help her mother.

Something must have happened.

She looks at me as though she's angry,

as though she knows I've lied to her.

I stand still and wait for them.

When they come close, the children trap me in a half circle.

"You thought you could fool us!" shouts Paul.

"We're not stupid.

We know if a Jew comes into your house, someone will die."

"And now that's happened!" yells a younger boy.
"As soon as your mother rented that house from my parents,
my brother Marcel got sicker and sicker.
Now he's dead . . . just like Jesus."

So our neighbor Marcel has died.
But that can't be my fault.
He's been sick since before I came to the village.
"I'm not Jewish!" I yell back.
"And how could I kill Jesus?
I'm not old enough."

Paul shouts, "Let's throw her in the water.
Shove her face under until she drowns."
The children all rush at me.

I remember what they did to the kittens.
I must run from the stream, get away fast . . .
anywhere!

I throw things—food, cider, rocks, flowers.
I use my sandals to beat back my enemies.
Then I run as far as I can get from the water.

The children catch me at the hedge next to the pasture.
I scratch, spit, kick, scream.
"You killed Marcel!"
I hear the children say.
"We'll tell the soldiers about you.
Throw her in the thorn bush!"

Thorns are better than water, I think.
Anything's better than drowning!

Paul and the other boys roll me in the thorns.
Then, like hunters done with their prey, they leave me.
Simone grabs her satchel.
Without even a glance back at me,
she herds the cows home across the fields.

Bruised and scratched all over,
I roll away from the thorns into thick grass.
I lie there and pant in the sun until my heart stops pounding.
Then I reach for a daisy and pull off its petals, one by one.
"They're gone, they're not gone, they're gone,"
I repeat to myself.
When the last petal tells me that they really are gone, I get up.

My blue cotton dress is torn.
I find my sandals and put them on.
Then I kneel down to pray.
"Thank you, God, for saving me.
Please watch over my mother."
I go back and find all the flowers I picked.
I'm going to take them straight to Mary.

On the way, I pass an old woman.
She's collecting twigs for a broom in her basket.
I might frighten her
with my tangled hair and torn dress,
covered with cuts and sores.
So I slip behind a tree
and wait until the old woman passes.

Why are all the children against me,
even my best friend, Simone? I wonder.
Maybe it's true that Marcel is dead,
but Mama said you can't live with tuberculosis forever.
I say all my prayers,
go to Mass,
and do well at my lessons.
What am I doing wrong?

I put my hand on the left side of my chest.
My star has been gone since I left Paris.
Did God punish me because I told a lie,
said that I was not Jewish?
But my mother told me to lie.
"It's a matter of life or death," she said.
And the priest tells us to obey our parents.

Will the children ever play with me again?
Will I have to walk to school all alone?
Or worse, will people tell the Nazis we are Jews?
Will they send Mama and me somewhere far away?
If that happens, will we ever come back?

The sun goes down.
Crickets start to sing,
and the trees raise their arms like spooky ghosts.
I shiver in my thin dress.

∾ Heartbroken ∾

At last!
Here's the door to Père René's barn.
In the cold twilight I fall on my knees.
Our Lady's calm presence
and the mooing of the cows soothes me.
I put my flowers in one of the clay pots
farmers use for liverwurst.
Streaks of silver pierce the half darkness . . .
the shiny paper we used to decorate the altar this morning.

Mary stretches out her arms to me,
loving as always.
"Our Lady of Mercy,"
I pray, "I'm scared.
You know I didn't kill your son, or Marcel.
Why did even Simone turn against me?
Forgive me for my lies.
My mother made me promise
never to say that we are Jews.
Please watch over us."

I am so tired, and the barn is warm.
I feel faint.
But I hear a noise behind me . . .

is someone else in the barn?

Not Paul, I hope!

No, but I do see the hunched figure of an old man

leaning on a carved stick.

He holds a lit candle in his right hand,

a hand with one too many fingers.

Père René, the kitten drowner, watches me.

His face looks as pale as a turnip

in the candlelight.

How long has he been here?

Did his huge ears hear my prayer?

Père René takes his time, then speaks.

"You are a sight, Odette . . .

oh, those children!

Always in fights over nothing.

Come now, child.

Make yourself useful.

Help me light the rest of the candles for Our Lady.

Then you'd better go on home.

Your mother's been looking for you everywhere.

If you hurry,

I'll give you some warm milk fresh from the cows.

That will get you on your way."

I find Mama sitting on her suitcase outside our cottage.

"We have nowhere to live," she says.

"Our landlord has taken away our cottage.

He accused me of being a Jew

because his son died.

I was so worried about you.

I didn't want you to come home

and find the house empty."

I tell Mama what has happened to me,

how the children accused me of being a Jew too,

and beat me up.

"Even Simone," I tell Mama, "even my best friend."

Mama makes room for me on the suitcase beside her.

I sit down and put my arms around her.

She puts her coat around my shoulders.

Together, we look up at the moon.

The moon gazes sadly back at us.

All we have is each other.

But Mama is a woman of action.

Even though it's late, she decides she must go,

right this minute,
to see the mayor in Saint-Fulgent.
She knows that he, like her, is a secret freedom fighter.

Mama tells me to hide in the cottage.
Soon she is back with the mayor.
"These people are not Jews,"
the mayor tells our neighbors.
"I know their family in Paris."
Because he is the mayor,
the villagers pretend to believe him.
And Mama and I pretend to forget
what the villagers have done to us,
throwing us out of our home, beating me up.
We move back into our cottage.

Mama gives a party to show the villagers
that we are still ready to be friends.
She bakes a cake and invites all the children,
even Paul and Simone.
Everyone comes.
I pretend to have a good time.
I keep all my sadness and anger buried inside,

like all my other secrets.
It's safer that way.

I can't stop being scared, though.
So scared that one day I stop going to school.
So scared that I even stop talking.

~ Mute ~

Some new city people have moved to our village.
They brought their son's books.
He's a student who's now in the army.
The family lets Mama borrow
as many books as she likes.
Every morning I take one.
I put some bread and apples in my backpack.
Then I go to the forest.

I climb a tree to get away from everything.
There, alone with the bats and owls,
I read all day long.
I am free from people who can't be trusted.
Only my mother is sad about this.
Sometimes I want to say something to comfort her,
but no words will come out.

Weeks of silence go by.
My mother tries to talk to me.
She asks me questions.
Sometimes I even think I have answered her.
She says I haven't.
It seems I can't say a word.

One day my mother tells me another secret.
She's reading some poetry, she says.
She thinks it's beautiful, but she's not sure.
She can't tell.

The poetry is written in French.
French does not "sing" to her like her own language, Yiddish.
Maybe if I read it out loud she'll be able to tell.
She sits on our doorstep in the sunshine.
I sit next to her.
I begin to read in silence.
Then the beauty of the words overtakes me.

And life, pounding our breasts like a drum,
I read aloud,
threatened to gush and overflow our souls. . . .

I read on and on.
The words roll off my tongue.
"Papa will love this," I say at last.

Mama's face shines.
I see Papa's face too, still wearing his army hat but smiling at me.

Distance has disappeared.
My mother, my father, and I are together again.

Poetry is stronger than the Nazis,
stronger than the war.
These words are so beautiful
they make me want to speak again.
The next day, I don't go to the forest.
I spend it reading poetry at home.
Sometimes I read aloud.
Day by day, I dare to say more.
After a while, Mama even talks me into going back to school.

I leave early and come home late
so that I won't have to walk with the village children.
But when I chant the litany with the other girls in class,
I feel like I'm reciting poetry.
That soaring inside me,
that's what it's like to be happy again.

~ My Guardian Angel ~

One morning when I push back the potato sack
that hangs over our front door in summer,
I find Simone waiting for me.
"Come and play with us, Odette," she says.
So I do.
But when we throw pickup sticks,
jump rope, or play ball,
I'm careful about what I do.
I'm still afraid of the village children.
What if a fight breaks out?
Will they make things my fault?

Père René is my new guardian angel.
He's always there.
He sharpens his scythe outside his cottage,
smokes his pipe with his dog at his feet,
and watches us,
ready at once to settle a fight.
I think I know why.
My six-fingered friend knows what it's like to be different.

~ Heart and Soul ~

Soon it will be harvest time, my favorite time of the year.
Men, women, and children sing together
while they load baskets with sweet grapes.
My favorite job is to follow the wheat harvester
and gather the shimmering stalks left in the grass.

In school, we learn about the five senses.
Our teacher asks us to write about our *pays*,
the place where we live.
We must write a poem about our *pays* in five parts,
one for each of the senses.
We can name all the sounds we like.
We can tell what smells, tastes, looks, or feels good to us.

I think about this on my way home from school.
I look at everything I pass on the road.
When I get to our village, I look at all the houses,
the winepress, even the black pond.
I take a walk through the forest to my favorite reading tree.
I stare.
I listen.
I touch.
I taste.

I smell.
Then I begin.

"I love my *pays*.
I love the sounds of the barnyard, the church bells,
and accordion music.
I love the smells of the flowers and the incense in church,
and the newly cut hay.
I love the taste of warm cow's milk and cool cider,
of blackberries and roasted chestnuts
and stew on winter nights.
I love the sight of lightning tearing up the sky,
of the golden flypaper shining in the sunlight.
I love the feel of the brook's fresh water between my toes,
and the weight of a ladybug on the back of my hand."

As I walk home,
I remember I have heard about a sixth sense.
When I ask Mama about it, she says that perhaps it is fear.
Fear is still with me.
I might be beaten again.
I might be drowned or my cat might be drowned.
Worst of all, Mama and I could be chased out of our village.
We could be sent on a long train journey, far away from France.

Reading helps me forget about fear.

I read everything from the *Farmer's Almanac* to fairy tales.

Poetry is still what I love best.

It doesn't matter if I don't understand it.

I can just listen to its music, or even read it to a cat or a cow.

I find a book by the Spanish saint Teresa of Avila.

It's almost like poetry.

On the first page, Saint Teresa says,

"We can think of our soul as a castle

made entirely of diamond or very clear crystal,

in which there are many rooms,

just as in heaven there are many dwelling places."

This is much grander than,

"The heart is like an apartment."

But Madame Marie lives in a tiny apartment.

Saint Teresa lived in a large convent.

So to her, the soul was like a castle.

Is the soul greater than the heart,

or is it just the same?

I'm not sure . . .

but I suspect it's the same.

People sometimes say they love with all their heart and soul.

So the heart and soul must be like twins,
helping people love all that's good and true,
no matter where they find it.

～ Mother's Day ～

Mama's sad and lonely.

No letters have come from Papa in a long time,

and she never hears from her family anymore.

One day, I see a pin in the shop window in Saint-Fulgent.

It glitters in sunset colors, pink and gold.

Mama would love it,

I just know she would.

And I know where Mama keeps our money.

I'll take some, just a little,

and I'll buy her a Mother's Day present.

It'll be a surprise!

After all, I earned some of it myself during harvest, didn't I?

Mama is outside at work in the garden.

I pry back the loose floorboard under the kitchen table.

I lift out the money jar.

I take out two silver coins, only two.

Then I put the jar and the board back.

I go to the shop to buy the pin.

The shopkeeper wraps it for me in pretty paper.

I make a Mother's Day card to go with it.

I spend a long time drawing violets on it, one by one.

Then I hide my card and present.

Will the violets remind Mama of the cologne she used in Paris?
I hope so . . . I can't wait for Sunday.

But on Saturday morning Mama counts our money.
"Odette," she says, "some money is missing."
I tell her I don't know anything about it.
"I think you do," says Mama.
"You are the only one who knows where I keep our money."
So I tell her it's true.
But I won't tell her what I did with it.
It's a secret.

Mama's eyes flash.
"I didn't raise you to be a liar," she says, "or a thief!"
A liar? A thief?
But all I'm doing is keeping a secret . . .
and Mama is the one who *taught* me to keep secrets.

Mama slaps my face, hard.
Bijou is shocked, and so am I.
The shape of Mama's hand stings my cheek.
It feels like fire.
But I don't say anything.

I just climb into my bed with Bijou.
I cuddle her,
and she licks and comforts me.
We both calm down.

The next morning, I bring Mama my Mother's Day present.
"Now I know where the money went," Mama says.
She tries to smile, but tears well up in her eyes.
Mama, who is so strong, who *never* cries, is sobbing.
I put my arms around her.
I don't tell her not to cry.
I know now crying can help you feel better.

~ Beautiful Bluma ~

Mama gets a letter that makes her hum with happiness.
Her old friend Bluma is coming for a visit.
She and Mama grew up in Poland together.
Bluma's husband is a French Christian,
and she speaks French with no accent.
Even so, her family is afraid . . .
someone might find out she is a Polish Jew.
Maybe, if she likes it in the country,
she will come and live with us.
Then Mama won't be so lonely.

Beautiful Bluma arrives,
in a silky blouse
and soft shoes.
Her eyelashes are the longest I've ever seen.
She has no children of her own
and makes me feel like her favorite niece.
Bluma has an expensive camera in a leather case.
She takes photographs of Mama and me,
of curving country lanes,
and of windmills and waterfalls.
At night, in the firelight,
we eat all the delicious dishes Mama has made for us.

Bluma has brought us chocolate too.
It's been so long since I tasted it,
I almost forgot its sweet bitterness,
and how it melts on my tongue.

Mama begs her friend to stay.
Bluma's face is pale in the dim light.
She *is* afraid, she tells us,
but she just can't leave the home she loves
and the husband she loves even more.
No, she will go back to Paris.

After only a few days,
we walk Bluma back to Saint-Fulgent.
The bus comes,
and she climbs on board.
She waves her handkerchief at us from the window
until we can't see her anymore.

A week later Mama gets a letter from Bluma's husband.
Bluma has been taken away,
like so many other Jews.
He asks if we can send her some food

at the camp where he thinks she is.

"Why didn't Bluma stay with us?" I ask.

"She would have been *safe* here!"

Mama sighs.

For a while she doesn't speak.

Then she says,

"Bluma was used to an easy life.

She couldn't give it up, not even for her own safety."

Then Mama puts down her letter and gazes out the window at pigs, rooting in the dirt.

"Life in the country was just too hard for her," she says.

～ The War Creeps Closer ～

Only one person in our village has a radio,
our landlord's son.
Mama and I go to his house
and crouch with him in front of his beat-up old radio.
We listen to scratchy sounds,
news of nearby battles.

The war is creeping closer and closer.
American and British soldiers land in Normandy,
and take part of France back from the Nazis.
Now they are blasting a strong submarine base,
only fifty miles away.
Bombs fall on Saint-Nazaire day and night.

Echoes of these bombs
reach as far as La Basse Clavalière.
I watch the lamp tremble over our table.
Sometimes it even swings back and forth.
I count how many times . . .
eight, nine, ten.
I tell myself if I get to twelve,
the war will be over.
But I never get quite that far.

Before long,
enemy soldiers fill Saint-Fulgent.
One day,
we hear Nazi soldiers march past our school.
They are singing a rowdy song.
My teacher closes the shutters
so we won't have to listen.
Then she closes the windows,
even though it's warm.
But we can still hear the song.

At first, my teacher looks sad.
But after a while,
her sadness shifts into anger.
She pounds one fist on her desk.
Then she pounds both fists.
We listen, and at last we understand.
She is pounding out the beat of "La Marseillaise,"
the French national anthem.
We begin to pound our desks too.
We're going to pound out the enemy soldiers,
pound out the sound of their song.
*"Arise, children of the Fatherland,
the day of glory has arrived. . . ."*

Our chests swell.

Like strong soldiers,

we battle bravely.

We'll win back freedom for our beloved country,

La Belle France,

or die trying.

~ The Soldiers Go Away ~

The Nazis leave our village at last!
The war is going badly for them.
The troops gather in the main square.
Their officer makes a speech.
He thanks the mayor for our village's hospitality.
Then he reaches forward to shake the mayor's hand.
"Never," says the mayor,
"would I shake hands with my country's enemy."
The officer's eyes darken with anger.
He marches off with his men.
Cars and trucks follow.
In the last one,
I see a goat.
She stands on the backseat,
her head stuck out the window.
Children chase after the car, laughing and cheering.
The goat watches them calmly.
She bats her eyelashes.

Within minutes, our houses and windows shake.
A deep rumble, a crash!
Are the soldiers bombing our village?
No, just our mayor's chateau.

The enemy officer had to repay our mayor's insult.

For refusing to shake hands,

his elegant mansion has been turned into a pile of rubble.

Two scared, stranded soldiers straggle into our village,

pushing carts packed with food.

They are lost.

"Can anyone show us which way the others went?" they ask.

"Oh, yes," says Mama.

She points in the direction of the woods,

where Resistance fighters hide.

In minutes, the enemy soldiers are back in the town square,

prisoners of our local young heroes.

Everyone gathers around the carts to see what's in them.

"Candy?" all the children ask.

"Is there any chocolate?"

When we find it,

we eat every last piece.

No one tries to stop us.

∾ Vive la France! ∾

"Hurry!" say the villagers.
"Don't miss the celebration in Saint-Fulgent.
News has come that Paris is free."

Mama drags me to Saint-Fulgent.
People dance in the streets.
"The war is almost over!" they shout.
France and its allies are winning.

What does this mean for us? I wonder.
Are Jews safe now?
What about Papa?

On the way home, Mama can't stop talking.
"No more cooking in a black iron pot.
No more straw mattresses or cottages filled with mice.
No more kneeling in church,
lugging water from the well,
pretending that your father does not exist."
She can't wait to get back to Paris,
to electric lights, running water, and indoor toilets.
My father and our neighbors and friends will all be there.
We'll join Jewish clubs; she'll read Yiddish books.

"And you, Odette, you'll have rubber boots, not *sabots.*
Instead of church on Sunday, we'll go to the public baths.
We'll *buy* soap, vinegar, wine, butter . . .
and skeins and skeins of wool.
We'll eat crepes in the winter, ice cream in the summer.
We'll go to museums, movies, and parks.
Paris has everything!
La Basse Clavelière has been just a nightmare."

It's true, we've had bad times here in the country,
that time I was beaten,
and we almost lost our home.
And I did lose my voice.
But we had *more* bad times in Paris, didn't we?
Besides, I don't mind the things Mama seems to hate.
I like getting water from the well and living in a cottage.
I love my *sabots* and going to church.
The country is my home now.
How can I leave it and go back to the city?
How can I leave the sweet cows and my pet cat, Bijou?
My forest, my fields and pastures, all my wildflowers?
How can I live without freedom,
in a place where I don't belong?

~ Adieu ~

I pray to all the saints, but no miracle can save me from Paris.
Mama's mind is made up.
As soon as she's sure the city is safe,
as soon as she's satisfied peace has come to stay in Paris,
she makes plans for us to return.
Even one extra day in the country is too many for her.

In the days before we leave,
I say good-bye to all my treasures, one by one.
I sit beside the shimmering ponds
and walk in the quiet forest for the last time.
I gather my last wildflowers and pat the gentle cows good-bye.
I light bright candles.
They flicker at the shrines of all the saints in church.
But I leave all my holy cards behind.
The only saint who can come with me is Joan of Arc.
She's a brave hero and is welcome everywhere in France.

The last creature I say good-bye to is Bijou.
Mama says she's a hunter.
She can take care of herself in the country better than in Paris.
Even so, I give Bijou's bowl
and the dangly string she likes to play with
to Simone.

I ask her to make sure my cat has water,
and to pet her until she purrs sometimes.
Simone says she will.

The morning Mama and I leave,
I give Charlotte to Simone,
to make sure she'll look after Bijou.
I don't trust Simone, not really.
I have never told her that I'm a Jew.
Mama and I agree about this.
We still keep it a secret here that we are Jewish . . .
a secret from everyone.

I scratch Bijou behind her ears, just the way she likes.
I stroke her one last time,
from her nose to the tip of her plumed tail.
Then I kiss her, right between her ears.
"*Adieu*," I whisper to her.
That's the French way to say,
"See you in heaven."

Monsieur Henri

∼ Home Again ∼

Paris is still a hungry place, Mama says.
So we fill suitcases and bags
with as much food as we can carry.
We board a train that chugs slowly over shaky bridges
 built on top of others that have been destroyed.
We rumble along through bombed-out villages.

I've heard the sound of bombs for years,
but now I see what they can do.
Houses hanging open.
Shops shattered.
Crumbled walls and toppled steeples.
We stop in a station to buy drinks.
I put my fingers into a hole blasted out of a stone archway.
If bombs can do this to stone,
what can they do to people?
I shudder.
I pull my hand away.

A journey that should take three hours now lasts three days.
By the time we reach Paris,
even Mama's not excited anymore.
We're both exhausted.

I trudge up the concrete steps of our *Métro* station.
I'm carrying almost as much weight as my mother is.
I don't want to climb up to the asphalt sidewalk.
If I could, tired as I am,
I'd travel backward all the way to my village right this minute.
But I do my best to lug the heavy bags on my back.
Mama calls out, "Odette, Odette! Look who's here!"

Can I be seeing things?
A large, rugged face appears before me . . . Monsieur Henri.
Everything else blurs, making way for his rough features.
How could he have known that Mama and I would be here,
just at this moment?
I can't believe our good luck.
But here he is, our own dear Monsieur Henri,
standing tall at the *Métro* exit.
At my mother's cry, he lumbers down to meet us.

"You've grown so big!" he says,
his huge hands on the tops of my shoulders.
He stands back for a moment and looks at me,
his kind, droopy eyes taking everything in.
Then Mama and I hand over all our bundles and bags.

He balances them on his strong back.
Light on my feet again,
I skip along the rue d'Angoulême behind him.

Once, when I was little,
I burned myself with boiling water.
Monsieur Henri carried me in his strong arms
to the pharmacist down the street.
Now he carries my village on his back.
Two and a half years ago—
what seems like a lifetime—
he walked me to the *Métro*.
He took me to the train station
to meet Cécile, Paulette, and Suzanne.
Now, looking like the Father Christmas of food,
he leads me back.
All the way down our street we go.
We pass the hardware store,
its bright pots and pans still shining in the sun.
We pass the café,
with people still reading their newspapers.
The convent appears, then the bakery, the factory.
At last, the little square with its benches, trees, and fountain.

Everything looks much the same,
but something is missing.
I'm not sure yet what that is.

Monsieur Henri heaves open the wooden door of our building.
I am almost afraid to look, but I do.
Yes, she's there!
In her tiny apartment at the end of the shiny tiled hallway,
the real Madame Marie looks up from her sewing machine.
She smiles her moon smile.
She rises from her work and holds out her arms to me.
I'm home and safe again in my godmother's arms.

That night, Mama and I move back into our apartment.
Madame Marie has saved it for us.
While we were gone, she used it as a hiding place for others.
But who would guess?
Our polished oak table, our beat-up pots and pans . . .
everything seems to smile at us.

Mama is full of joy seeing all her worn-out treasures.
But I look at my toys with new eyes.
My rubber ball looks babyish to me now.

So do my books, puzzles, and wind-up toys.
All I will keep
is my flowered parasol.

Our next-door apartment is silent.
What happened to the pretty young girl who lived there?
She was the girlfriend of one of the enemy soldiers.
Did the French arrest her? Mama wonders.
Did they shave her head,
force her to march in shame through the streets?
"Don't worry," says Madame Marie.
"I found a safe place for her out in the country.
Yvette wasn't a bad girl, just young and poor.
She liked going to the opera
on the arm of a young man in uniform.
Not many young Frenchmen were around during those days."

On my bed that night,
I find the blanket made by Madame Marie.
It feels like an old friend.
But wait . . . something's wrong!
The holy medals are all gone.
Someone has cut them off.

My childhood protectors, St. Christopher and St. Michael,
what happened to them?
But I am too tired to think about this for long.
Instead, I wrap my old friend around me
and drift into deep, delicious dreams.

In the morning, I push open the shutters once again.
I lean out and look at the square.
The nuns in white-winged bonnets still sail across it.
The Thinker sits in his same place too.
Does he ever wonder about Papa, like I do?
I see that stores once having Jewish names
now have French ones.
Only a few gypsies are left.
The dark-eyed children peek out
from behind their mothers' long skirts.

I know what's missing!
Our neighborhood looks like a black-and-white photograph.
Color hasn't come back yet to Paris.

∿ Growing Up ∿

Of the two rooms that make up our apartment,
my favorite was once the living room.
Before we went away,
I sat under the round table there and played with my toys.
But now I spend almost all my time in the bedroom.
The tall bookcase there goes from the floor up to the ceiling.
My favorite books are four fat ones,
The Encyclopedia of Learning.
Long ago, my father read to me
and showed me the pictures in these books.
Now I read them myself.

The *Encyclopedia* is different
from the books I read in the Vendée.
No poetry or fiction is found in an encyclopedia.
It's all about facts—
science, history, and geography.
I study the photographs, the maps, and the charts.
I can see why my father loved his *Encyclopedia* so much!
Now that I'm older,
I'm going to read as much of it as I can.
I'm hungry to learn everything,
just like my father did.

We keep our clothes in the curvy old armoire.
Inside is a silvery mirror.
I spend hours looking at myself in that mirror.
I try out my mother's scarves,
and if she isn't home,
I put on her face powder and lipstick.
I experiment with glamorous hairstyles too.
I study my face from different angles.

Everyone says I'm growing up,
becoming a woman.
What kind of woman will I be?
Will I be beautiful, like Bluma?
Will I be brave, like Mama?
Will I be strong, like Madame Marie?
Will I be kind, like Madame Raffin?
I want to be *all* these things.

———

∾ New Friends ∾

School in Paris smells the same . . .
waxed floors, glue, new books.
Some of the same children are there too.
Others have disappeared.
No one calls me names anymore, though,
and no one dares to beat me up.

Coming home one day,
I open the door and turn on the light.
Something leaps under the table . . . a yellow kitten!
No one knows where he came from.
Mama and I both miss Bijou,
so we fuss over the yellow kitten.
We offer him fresh milk,
bits of buttered bread,
a piece of ham.
The kitten purrs and falls asleep in my arms.
What shall we name him?
Mama likes Zola, after a famous French writer.
I like Minou, slang for "pussycat."
But one day when I get home from school,
before we have a chance to decide,
he's gone.

I run down and ask Madame Marie if she's seen my kitten.
She asks if our window is open . . . uh-oh.
It is.
"Go look in the square," she says.
"Maybe he climbed a tree and can't get down."
She's right, my yellow kitten's in the square.
He's climbing the statue of *The Thinker.*
I lift him down gently and take him home.
We decide to name him Tarzan, after the movie hero.
I adore him, but he's a troublemaker.

First of all, he's always disappearing.
He finds his way back home,
but then Mama complains that he's a fussy eater.
He only likes bread with butter or pâté.
Mama says we can barely feed ourselves.
Tarzan has to change his ways
or find another place to live.

Pretty soon, he does.
I comb the neighborhood but can't find him.
My heart is broken.
Mama says Tarzan's probably exploring a park

or playing games with other cats.
But what if he's lying hurt in the street somewhere?
All I want to do is hold and pet him again.
"Having Tarzan was fun for a while," Mama says,
"but he's gone now, Odette.
You have to forget about him."

I try.
I keep going to school,
and before long, I make a new friend.
Esther's been hiding in the country, just like I was.
We both love to window shop,
eat ice cream cones,
and explore the streets in our neighborhood.
I never knew there were so many things to see . . .
street entertainers, chalk artists, and pushcart vendors.
It's like a circus!

I've almost forgotten about Tarzan when,
months later,
I pass an elegant apartment building.
The street door is open for movers.
Curious, I walk in to see what it looks like.

Voilà Tarzan,
strutting across the courtyard.
He's bigger, fatter, furrier, but I know it's him.
My first thought is to kidnap him and take him home,
but if I did I know he'd run away again.
Then I wouldn't even know where he was.
No, I know he's better off here,
spoiled by some rich family.

I lean over and rub my fingers through Tarzan's thick fur.
He licks my knuckles.
Does he remember me?
His amber eyes don't say.
One last scratch behind the ears,
and I stand and walk out of the courtyard.
I can't stay home after school with a cat anymore.
Esther's waiting for me.

~ Au Revoir, Madame Marie ~

"Did you hear, Odette?
Madame Marie and Monsieur Henri are moving."
I drop my book.
"Moving away?" I ask.
Mama nods and goes on chatting.
Her eyes are on her knitting,
so she doesn't see the shock in mine.
How can this be?

So many people in my life have come and gone . . .
my father, my aunts and uncles, my cousins.
But Madame Marie has always been there.
I've counted on her,
even when I was far away,
to take care of me.
How could my godmother leave my mother and me?
I run downstairs to see her.
"Is it true?" I ask.

My godmother beams at me.
Yes, she and Henri have found a larger apartment.
It comes with an easier job too, looking after a small factory.
"We're getting older now, Odette.

It's a good place for Henri and me.
It's not too far away,
and you will always be welcome with us."
My godmother is so happy,
she makes me want to feel happy too.
But I can't, not quite.
I will miss her so much,
even though I know things have changed between us.

"You're such a big girl now," she always says,
as if I grew up on purpose during my time away.
We never talk in the same way, either.
She always listens,
and I can tell she's impressed
when I tell her about all I've learned.
Did she know, I ask her one day,
that humans are related to chimpanzees?
But when I try to tell her other things,
I'm a little shy.
I don't know what to say,
how to begin to tell my godmother about my feelings now.
I'd like her to know that I'm not so sure I like getting bigger,
that I don't feel ready for it.

People are always talking about the Resistance.
Many people gave their lives for France during the war.
Some of them were only teenagers,
a few years older than I am now.
Would I have the courage to do that when I'm a teenager?
I'd like to ask my godmother,
but I can't find the words.
If only she would ask me what the heart is like again,
so I can show her I remember.
But she never asks.

I give Madame Marie a hug,
to show her I'm happy for her.
I don't trust my voice
to tell her how much I'll miss her.
So I simply close the door on her little apartment,
the place where I have always been so safe and so happy,
the place where she saved my life.
I look back through the sheer-curtained window.
My godmother sews as always,
and the clock ticks behind her.
I peer back at her, take in every detail . . .
her long gray hair coiled in a bun,

the concentration on her face,
her careful fingers poised at the machine.

Even though she's going away
I'll carry this image of her always.

~ Lost and Found ~

For Jews, all of France has become a gigantic Lost and Found.
They look for their children in orphanages, and convents.
They try to get their jobs, apartments, and businesses back.
Decent people return everything.
The greedy fight over what they want to keep.
Lives come together slowly,
like the pieces of a giant puzzle.

Three pieces of that puzzle
are Aunt Georgette, Uncle Hirsch, and my cousin Sophie.
When all of them come back—
Aunt Georgette and Sophie from their cousin's farm,
and Uncle Hirsch from the army—
they find their apartment stripped bare.
Still, they say they're happy to be alive.

My uncle sings as he makes suits at his sewing machine,
and my aunt sings along with him.
Steam from her ironing or from a stew she's stirring
clouds around her.
She listens to the news my uncle brings home . . .
a neighbor has found a good job,
the butcher shop has fresh meat again,

a friend's daughter will marry the local shoemaker.

Wonderful! Aunt Georgette says.

My uncle whistles happily,

as if he made these things happen all by himself.

Sophie and I drink tea and nibble on paper-thin matzoh bread.

Matzoh's not allowed in my home.

It's connected somehow to religion . . .

I have no idea how.

I envy my cousin.

Whatever she does seems to make her parents happy.

They love to see her in the beautiful dresses

they make for her.

She can listen to Edith Piaf on the radio all day long

if she wants to.

Not me . . . I have to study.

Sophie sleeps in the dining room alone at night too.

I still sleep in the bedroom with my mother.

I think about my other cousins—

Sarah, Serge, Charles, Henriette, and Maurice—

all the time.

At last I ask Mama what happened to them,

and to Aunt Miriam and Uncle Motl.

Mama says she ran to their apartment on Black Thursday,
the day that the police came to arrest us.
The door was open.
Mama froze in that spot, unable to move.
On the table, a knife in the bread,
halfway through the loaf.
An untouched glass of milk.
On one chair, Sarah's wrinkled dress,
waiting to be ironed.
In a corner, Henriette's shoes.
Did Henriette leave barefoot?
We'll never know.
She and everyone else are gone.

Mama talked to the neighbors.
Uncle Motl hid in a tool shed, they said.
That's what the Jewish leaders told men to do.
They thought only men would be arrested.
But when my uncle heard his wife scream and his children cry,
he came out.
The police took them all away.

Mama takes a folded scrap of paper from the drawer.
It is a letter from eleven-year-old Serge.

Dear Auntie,

Henriette and I are alone. Our parents are gone.
Sarah went away to one camp with my mother, and
Charles to another with my father. You are the only one
who can help us. I don't know what to do now for my
little sister Henriette. She cries for Mama all the time,
and doesn't want to eat. The food is terrible, rotten
cabbage soup. Please send us something to eat. Also,
please send me a beret. They have shaved our heads
because of the lice, and it makes me feel so strange, like
a criminal. I would feel so much better with a beret.
Your nephew,
Serge

Mama says she tried to send Serge and Henriette some food.
But she never heard from anyone in the family again.
"Your aunt and uncle and all your cousins are gone," she says.

"Gone?" I say.
"But maybe they'll come back."

Mama shakes her head.
"They're not coming back, Odette," she says.

"They're gone forever."
Like my father? I wonder.
But I don't dare ask that question out loud.
I see how eagerly Mama still checks the mail,
how her shoulders slump sometimes,
afterward.
She's still waiting.
Waiting for a letter from Papa.
We haven't had one since we came back to Paris.

I decide I must look for my cousins myself.
I don't tell Mama.
I cross the big boulevard.
I pass the bakery.
I walk down their alley.
The smell is the same: urine and cabbage.
All the windows in the dreary courtyard stare at my back.

The caretaker peers out at me from behind her lace curtains.
A big man comes out of my aunt's apartment.
He knows nothing about my cousins, he says.
He has lived in the apartment for two years.
Did anyone come back, anyone at all? I ask.

"Never!" he replies.
He goes back into the apartment and slams the door.
I stare at the door, hoping to hear Serge's violin,
Henriette's giggle,
Uncle Motl's knitting machine.
Silence.

The caretaker opens her door.
"What do you want?" she asks.

"My cousin's violin," I say.
She shuts the door.
But I come back, again and again.
Each time I ask her the same thing,
"Where is Serge's violin?"

"How should I know?" she says.
"That family's long gone.
Go away.
You're a pest."

Maybe I can find Serge's violin in a pawnshop, I decide.
I window-shop at all the pawnshops in the neighborhood.

I never saw so many violins!
I was sure I would know my cousin's violin anywhere,
but I was wrong.
Can I ask my mother to describe it?
No.
Talk of my cousins brings her too much grief.

Anyway, what would I do if I found Serge's violin?
I don't have any money to buy it.
Still, I choose three or four violins.
I go back and visit them often,
to make sure no one else has bought them.
I'm not sure which is the magical one,
the one that leaned on Serge's shoulder.
But at least I have some idea where it is.

If Serge comes back, he won't be disappointed.
When he knocks on our door, I'll take him to see the violins.
I'm sure he'll remember which one is his.

～ Survivors ～

Everywhere in Paris, I see people wearing black—
women in black dresses, men with black armbands.
Mama says they're mourning people they loved,
people who died in the war.
"They survived, but they're still suffering.
If you speak to them, speak gently."

Mama has a surprise for me . . . our friend Bluma is back.
The train taking her to a camp in Poland
was bombed by the Resistance . . .
she escaped.
Now she's home in Domont,
her sleepy small town outside Paris.
Mama and I go to visit her.
Bluma's home is like her, elegant, serene.
Her husband, Edmond, asks us not to stay too long.
Bluma's still frail, he says.

She had to stay in a camp near Paris, a place called Drancy.
"It was a terrible camp," Bluma tells us.
"Dirty, overcrowded, nothing to eat."
She shakes her head.
"I was so foolish.

I should have stayed with you in the country."
Mama puts her arm around Bluma's thin shoulders.
I stroke her pale hand.
No one says,
It's true, you should have stayed.
But the words seem to be there,
hanging in the air.

On the train on the way home,
Mama tells me that my cousins—
Serge, Charles, Henriette, and Sarah—
stayed in the camp at Drancy too.
"That was before they were sent to Poland,"
Mama says.
She shakes her head.
"For all we suffered, Odette," she says,
"you and I were lucky to be in the Vendée."
She's right, I know.
But I couldn't be more surprised to hear Mama say it.

Summer comes,
and Mama signs me up for a Jewish youth group.
One awful day, our leaders take us to see Drancy.

We wander around the empty camp.

Our footsteps echo off the concrete walls and floors.

The guide tells us people had to sleep on those floors.

How could they? I wonder.

It must have been so cold, so hard.

On an outside wall, I see letters scrawled by a child's hand.

One word: "Mama."

In the dirt, I spy a child's toothbrush.

I want to pick it up,

but I don't dare.

Like Mama said,

I'm one of the lucky ones,

one of the survivors.

I never had to suffer like the owner of that toothbrush did.

Somehow I don't have the right

even to touch it.

My friend Leon comes back to our neighborhood.

He was the tall, strong boy

who lifted me onto his shoulders to see the gypsy's goat

the day I got my orange from Marshal Pétain.

He's eighteen now but so weak he can't even stand up.

Mama says he was in a camp where people were starved.
Leon, who always had a smile
and friendly words to say to me,
barely has the strength to speak.

I visit Leon every day after school.
Our visits are always the same.
He lifts the corner of his pillow
and offers me a piece of the American gum he keeps there.
Then he asks me a question, the same one every day:
"What did you learn in school today?"

I always save up something special to tell him.
He's so interested in my answers.
I can tell by the way his large, dark eyes follow mine.
I collect information for him
the way I once
collected mushrooms and berries in the Vendée.
Leon likes poetry, especially.
I memorize poems for him.
Though nobody says it,
I know he'll die soon.
I want to bring him as much beauty as I can.

On my way to see Leon, I walk past Saint Joseph's Church.
I want to go in, but I can't.
Now that I am back in Paris, I must be a Jew again.
Being a Christian would make me a bad Jew.
I want to talk to God about this problem.
I want to ask him what I should do.
But even though God lives with many Jews,
he doesn't live in my home.
I can't talk to my mother about God or prayer.
Now that we don't pretend to be Christians anymore,
she doesn't want to hear anything about it.

When I arrive in Leon's room one day,
it's even quieter than usual.
My heart beats quicker
as I walk toward his bed.
Has death already come to take my friend?
No, Leon is still with me.
He doesn't speak, but he looks at me.
His eyes are larger than ever, a deeper and more urgent brown.
They seem to want to say something terribly important.
I want to ask them questions too,
questions I never dared ask Leon out loud.

How terrible was it in the camp?
What's it like to die?
What does it mean to be a Jew?
Should I be one?

Leon's eyes read mine and answer me.

The camp was a nightmare.
Dying here, at home, is a gift.
To be a Jew is to know death and to love life.
Be a Jew like me.

What else can my eyes answer?

Yes, I will.
Of course I will.
I promise.

Before long, Leon's stare softens and his eyelids slip shut.
I close the door softly behind me.
Shwush.
Click.

~ My People ~

One spring day, Europe's Lost and Found
finds something to return to French Jews . . .
a small box.
The box contains the ashes of Jews who died in terrible places,
places called concentration camps.
No one really knows for sure,
but they might be the ashes of our friends and relatives.
We will bury the box at Père Lachaise Cemetery.

Père Lachaise is near where my cousins used to live.
But when I go there, I always think of Madame Marie.
She spent her Sundays at the cemetery.
She liked the tall trees, the fine statues,
the prowling cats.
She paid her respects to the famous at Père Lachaise,
like the writers Balzac and Molière.
Her favorites were the actress Sarah Bernhardt
and the medieval lovers Abelard and Heloise.
But she never limited herself to them . . . oh, no!
She liked to see that all the tombs were in order.
If she found one that wasn't, she tidied it.
Straightened an old photograph, lined it up on an altar,
dusted cobwebs away with Monsieur Henri's handkerchief.

Cemeteries were my godmother's hobby.

But there are huge crowds of people at Père Lachaise today . . .

Madame Marie will not be here.

She stays away from crowds.

I miss her so much I ache inside.

Sometimes, in the middle of my days in Paris, I feel confused.

I still wonder who I *really* am

and where I *really* belong!

In the city?

In the country?

At church?

Or at my Jewish youth group?

If only I could talk to my godmother about this.

But since she moved away,

I don't see her as often as I would like.

If I did see her and could tell her I'm not sure who I really am,

I think I know what she would say.

"The war is over now.

You are the Jewish child of Jewish parents.

You don't have to be Christian anymore.

In the eyes of God,

it doesn't matter where you live.
It's *how* you live that is important.
Be a decent person who lives by her heart."
But how do I do this?
How do I live by my heart?

Mama and I come to Père Lachaise early.
We're there when the leaders of the march arrive,
the skinniest men and women I've ever seen.
These silent survivors gather in the thin rain.
They are Jews who returned from the concentration camps.
Their worn striped uniforms
look like pajamas that are too big for them.
Their eyes are much too large.
They walk as if they only half remember how to do it, or why.
They seem sacred . . . set apart from ordinary people.
Only one outsider, God Himself,
could ever understand their thoughts and feelings.

Finally the leaders disappear into the cemetery,
carrying the small wooden box.
It's the size of a baby's coffin.
Mama and I, with groups of people our own ages, follow them.

We walk in silence under the weeping sky,

past sorrowful stone angels.

Some of us weep too.

Around us are grand tombs

carved with the last names of single families.

First names, dates, and places have been carefully recorded.

But all we have left of our loved ones is this small box of ashes.

It may be these ashes are not even theirs.

Suddenly, out of the crowd, a woman rushes up.

She reaches for me,

draws me to her, and hugs me until it hurts.

I don't know her.

I've never even seen her before.

I'm sure she doesn't know me.

But here she is, holding me as if she'd lost me,

missed me terribly,

and then found me again.

Should I push her away?

Should I call Mama?

In pain and joy the woman cries, "I had a daughter like you!"

Was her daughter my age?

Did she look like me?
The mother repeats again and again,
"I had a daughter like you!"
She strokes my hair, presses my face into her chest.

My heart tells me what to do . . .
it's so simple.
Let this woman be your mother.
Be her daughter.
So I hug her.
I stroke her back as a lost-and-found daughter would.
I am every Jewish daughter who has died.
She is every Jewish mother who has lost a child.
Slowly, she begins to run out of tears.
Her friend takes her by one hand.
Covering her eyes with the other,
the woman staggers away.

I lie awake that night in my bed,
the bed that's grown too small for me.
I finger my yellow blanket, thinking.
I belong to my family.
To Mama, of course.

To Papa too, if he ever returns.

To my godmother, Madame Marie, and to Monsieur Henri.

But the tears of the woman I met today

have washed away every speck of dust in my heart,

every trace of fear.

I'm a child of my family,

a child of France.

But, more than these,

my heart tells me now

I'm a child of my people.

The dead we buried today in the small wooden box,

the living brothers and sisters who have survived.

I don't need to hide anymore,

and I don't want to keep any more secrets.

Secrets stand in my way.

They stop me from knowing who I am.

I am a Jew.

I'm sure of it.

And I will always be one.

∼ The Present ∼

It's a hot, dull day in July,
just before school lets out for the summer.
Our class is copying a map
when a knock sounds at the schoolroom door.
It's the skinny new caretaker,
the one who's taken Madame Marie's place.
She speaks to my teacher.
My teacher smiles
and calls me forward.
"Your father has returned," she tells me.
"You may go home to see him."

I take my time walking there.
I should feel happy, I know.
The trouble is,
I don't really know who my father is anymore.
I was only a little girl
when he went away.
Except for that one visit in the hotel room,
I haven't seen him in five years.
We haven't had a letter from him
in more than a year.
What will we have to say to each other?

He doesn't know me and I don't know him.
What if he doesn't like me?
What if I don't like him?
Will we have to live together anyway?

Many of my friends,
including Esther,
have lost mothers or fathers,
brothers or sisters.
Now our family will be whole again.
I'll be different from my friends.

Slowly, I open the door to our apartment.
The electricity is turned off in the daytime.
A man sits in the shadows at our table,
wearing a soldier's uniform and cap.
I stand near the table with my back to the wall.
The man tries to talk to me.
I try to answer.
Out of the man's pocket comes a chocolate bar.
But even the enemy soldiers
tried to make friends with children, didn't they?
They offered us candy too.

The man acts just like every other soldier.
How can I be sure he's my father?

The man begins to tell me stories.
He tells me the Red Army liberated his prison camp.
What is the Red Army?
Did the soldiers wear red uniforms?

The man ran away through vast forests
with other Jewish prisoners.
The war was over, but they were far from France.
They had to walk most of the way back,
through empty bombed-out villages and farms.
All along the way,
they heard gunshots
and the sound of unmilked cows, mooing in pain.
His journey home took eight months.
As the man speaks,
I begin to remember my father,
the man who read stories to me so long ago.
I'm hungry for more details,
for richer stories.
"How did you survive?" I ask.

"We'd find food," he said,
"chickens and vegetables on abandoned farms.
We'd make ourselves a feast and rest . . .
then move on."
I nod, asking for more.
"And I had poetry,"
he says,
"reading poems helped me survive."

Poetry?
So the beauty of words kept him alive,
just as it comforted Leon,
and just as it gave me my voice back!

"I have a present for you," the man says,
opening his knapsack.
"In one empty house,
I found a jewelry box.
In it was a necklace,
a single strand of small pearls,
just right for a young girl.
I hadn't seen anything so beautiful for so long
that I decided to put it in my knapsack for you."

For me?
So this man brought home
a pearl necklace for me?
He must be my real father
or why would he do that?
No one else I know has a real pearl necklace.
How will I feel when I wear it?
Proud?
Embarrassed?

"But the next morning I changed my mind,"
the man says.
"I thought about the girl who owned it.
What if she came back?"

My heart sinks.
My fingers have already touched the smooth pearls.
I've already seen them shining around my neck.
And now they're gone.

The man reads my face.
"Never mind," he says.
"Later on, I found something even better."

Even better?

What could that be? I wonder.

My eyes travel to the man's brown knapsack.

Is it the one Madame Marie made for my papa?

I just can't remember.

The man begins to take things out.

Clothing, food . . . a worn-out dictionary!

The dictionary has lost its cover,

so I can't tell if it's the blue one.

But maybe this really is my papa after all!

Who else would carry a dictionary for five long years?

At last the man finds the package he's looking for.

He hands it to me.

The package is small,

but too big for jewelry, I think.

I can barely breathe.

Slowly, I unwrap it.

Inside is a fine leather notebook.

It looks like a diary

but with no lock or key,

so it's not a place for keeping secrets.

I run my fingers across the paper,
smooth as the skin of a newborn baby.
I smell the leather,
rich and spicy.
"What's this for?" I ask.
"For you to write in,"
the man replies.
For me to write in?
I lean over and kiss him on the cheek.
"Thank you, Papa," I say.

Yes, telling my story is what I must do.
I'll write it down here
in the most beautiful words I can find.
The story of bombs and broom closets,
of stars and soldiers,
of cats and cousins,
of family and friends,
of heaven and hell.

The story of all the secrets I kept . . .
and the story of my lost-and-found heart.

~ TIMELINE ~

January 1933

Adolf Hitler and his Nazi Party come to power in Germany. Jews in that country begin to be excluded from public life.

November 1934

Odette Melspajz (later, Meyers) is born in Paris to Jewish parents of Polish origin, Berthe and George Melspajz.

September 1939

Hitler invades Poland as a first step toward conquering all of Europe. France and England declare war on Germany.

November 1939

George Melspajz joins the French army.

June/July 1940

France is defeated, and the German occupation begins. Marshal Phillippe Pétain is named head of the Vichy government in France, which collaborates with the Nazis.

May, August, December 1941

The first large-scale roundups of Jews take place. Only men are arrested. They are kept in camps in France.

March 1942

The first foreign-born Jews in France are deported to death camps in Poland.

May/June 1942

French Jews over the age of six are required to wear yellow stars on their clothing. They are forbidden to go to parks, restaurants, libraries, and other public places.

July 1942

Nearly thirteen thousand foreign-born Jews are arrested in Paris and deported to death camps. Odette escapes to the Vendée.

January 1943

The first roundups of French-born Jews begin.

March 1943

Berthe Melspajz joins Odette in hiding in the Vendée.

June 1944

After many sea and air battles, Allied forces invade France in a final, successful effort to defeat the Nazis.

August 1944

Paris is liberated.

October 1944

Berthe Melspajz and Odette return to Paris.

April 1945

Hitler commits suicide.

May 1945

Germany surrenders. The war in Europe is over. The death camps in Poland are liberated, and surviving Jews begin to try to return to their homes.

July 1945

George Melspajz returns home.

Odette's Secrets is classed as a work of fiction, but it is based very closely on a true story. Here is how it came to be. One late August afternoon a few years ago, I was walking through the Marais, an old Jewish neighborhood in Paris, with my husband. We passed an elementary school with a bronze plaque. The plaque honored the memory of the Jewish children, students at the school, who had been deported from France during World War II. I put my hand on the warm stone of the school, thinking of those children. Who were they? What were their lives like in France during the war?

I began to read about life in Paris during World War II, especially about the life of French Jews. I learned that 11,400 children were deported. Most died in concentration camps in Eastern Europe. But more children survived in France than in any other European country, 84 percent. How did this happen?

Most were hidden in homes, convents, monasteries, farms, and schools all over the country. To stay successfully hidden, children had to reinvent themselves, to deny their families and their identity and "become" French

Christian children. How in the world were children able to do this? I wondered. And what was it like for them to readjust to reality after the war?

In October I was still thinking over these questions when I was invited to the American Library in Paris to read my book *The Costume Copycat* at the library's annual Halloween party. After all the pirates and princesses went home, I went upstairs to browse in the stacks. And there, by chance, I found *Doors to Madame Marie*, the autobiography of Odette Meyers, a woman who had been one of those hidden French children during the war.

I became fascinated by Odette's story. I pored over the photographs of her and her family and friends, read and reread her adventures, especially the passages where she described what it was like to switch selves, not once but twice, both in the remote countryside of the Vendée where she hid and then back in Paris again after the war. I visited the street where Odette's family lived, and sat in the square opposite their building, studying the door and the window of their apartment above. I walked up the street, as Odette did, imagining her holding the hand of her beloved Monsieur Henri as he led her past the French policemen sent to arrest her and her mother on Black Thursday, July 16, 1942. Did the café and the convent she mentioned in her book look the same then? Where was her school? I explored the alleyway where her dear cousins lived, the cousins who were deported from France weeks after their arrest and never returned. I strolled in the park where Odette played, and in the cemetery where she came face-to-face with who she was after the war.

One night, I told my husband Odette's story. Together, we took the *Métro* to the 11th *arrondissement* and stood outside Odette's apartment building. "I *so* wish I could go inside!" I said, looking at the heavy oak door at the front of the building, a solid street door of the type that is always locked.

"Let's see if we can," my husband said, and pressed his fingertips against the door. It swung open! In moments we were standing in the tiled hallway where Odette played with her red rubber ball. At the end was the tiny apartment of her godmother, Madame Marie, the place where Odette and her mother hid in her broom closet when the police came at dawn to arrest them. I couldn't believe my luck . . . the opening of that door seemed like a sign. I just *had* to write for children the story of Odette's remarkable life.

I had grown up in a neighborhood with many immigrants near Detroit just after World War II. War stories, including some involving the Holocaust, were part of the fabric of our lives. But I had never before heard the story of how children saved themselves from death through their own courage and ingenuity. This was the story I wanted to tell.

But how? Odette had lived and prospered as a mother, a teacher, and a writer, but she had died in 2002. Still, I knew she had a son, Daniel, and he lived in Paris.

I found her son's number in the Paris telephone directory. With my heart in my mouth, I dialed the number. I left a message, explaining who I was and what I hoped to do. Then I waited. A few days later, Daniel called me back and invited me to lunch in his sunny apartment on the rue Rambuteau. He listened to my request and made his decision almost immediately. His mother, he said, had often talked in schools and libraries to children about her wartime experience. He was sure she would want her story to live on. As her literary executor, he gave me permission to use the facts of her life as the basis of a book for children.

I was thrilled but wanted to learn as much as I could about Odette and her family and experiences first. Daniel gave me his grandmother's autobiography and some of his mother's poems. He showed me film clips and more family photographs. He also told me that although Odette and her three friends thought they were the only Jewish children in the small village where they lived in the remote country area of the Vendée, in fact, more than forty children were hidden there by local families.

I decided I needed to visit the Vendée. I took the train to Nantes, as Odette did at the time of her escape from Paris. All the way I studied the farmhouses, the villages, and the train stations passing by. What was there in 1942? Did Odette see it as I did? Then I drove to Chavagnes-en-Paillers, the first village where Odette was hidden in plain sight during the war. My husband and I were standing outside the house where she lived when a kindly old man appeared at the upstairs window and invited us in. He was Jacques Raffin, who had been one of the children of the family that had sheltered Odette. He showed me the garden where they had played together on the swing and fed the pigeons. Afterward, we visited the school Odette attended with her friends Cécile and Paulette, and the church where she went to Mass every Sunday. Finally, we went to the hamlet where Odette and her mother lived together under assumed names. We saw the forest and the square where she played hide-and-seek and hopscotch, the pathway she took walking to school in the town of Saint-Fulgent. The fields, the cows, and the cottages were all still there. Now that I had seen as much of Odette's wartime world as I could, I was ready to write.

I wrote and rewrote Odette's story many times before I was satisfied with it. At first I attempted to write it as a straight biography. This version seemed too dry. Then, with Daniel's permission, I tried writing it in first person, in free verse, imagining insofar as I was able the childhood voice of Odette, the poet-to-be. I imagined details such as the name Odette's beloved doll might have had, and the actual words that might have made up conversations to which Odette and her mother had alluded in their writings. Now the book became a work of fiction rather than nonfiction, but I hoped this might make it more accessible to today's children. When I was finally satisfied with my manuscript, I gave it to my agent, Steven Chudney, whose own father had been hidden on a Christian farm in Poland during World War II. He found just the right editor for *Odette's Secrets*—Melanie Cecka, whose sensitive suggestions helped shape the book still further.

Odette Meyers's life, like that of her fellow writer Anne Frank, was threatened with extinction. But unlike Anne, she went on to live and thrive. She moved with her parents to California after the war, graduated from college, married the poet Bert Meyers, and raised two children, Daniel and Anat. She taught French literature and made many devoted friends. And she always made it a point to share the story of her childhood in schools, churches, and temples; in her autobiography; and in her contribution to the award-winning 1984 film *The Courage to Care*. My hope is that today's children, including her grandson Sacha, will come to know her life and times, her spirit and determination to survive, through this book.

∽ ACKNOWLEDGMENTS ∽

My greatest debt of gratitude in writing this book is to Daniel Meyers, Odette's son. From the start, he welcomed me into his home and was always generous with his time and help. Without his cooperation and assistance, I would have been unable to write *Odette's Secrets*.

I am also especially grateful to my husband, George Macdonald. His support and enthusiasm for my work is unfailing.

Steven Chudney, my agent, has been my steadfast ally in seeing *Odette's Secrets* on its road to publication. Melanie Cecka gave the manuscript the benefit of her thoughtful, sensitive, and intelligent editing. Brett Wright's courtesy and diplomacy made it easy to accept his astute suggestions. These two editors made me happy my book had found a home at Bloomsbury. Last but not least, my friends and fellow writers, including Louise Borden, Trish Marx, Paula Panich, and Richard Peck, read the manuscript at different stages along the way and offered much encouragement.

Thank you all from the bottom of my heart.